HAVE COURAGE,
HAZEL GREEN

Also by ODO HIRSCH

Hazel Green
Something's Fishy, Hazel Green
Bartlett and the Ice Voyage
Bartlett and the City of Flames
Bartlett and the Forest of Plenty

HAVE COURAGE,
HAZEL GREEN

by

ODO HIRSCH

BLOOMSBURY
CHILDREN'S
BOOKS

JF Hirsch
Hirsch, Odo.
Have courage, Hazel Green!

Published by Bloomsbury Publishing, New York, London, and Berlin
Distributed to the trade by Holtzbrinck Publishers

Library of Congress Cataloging-in-Publication Data
Hirsch, Odo.
Have courage, Hazel Green / Odo Hirsch.
p.   cm.
Summary: When she overhears one of the tenants in her apartment building
verbally abusing the hard-working caretaker, Mr. Egozian, Hazel Green
determines to find a way to teach the unpleasant tenant a lesson.
ISBN-10: 1-58234-659-3 • ISBN-13: 978-1-58234-659-5
[1. Prejudices—Fiction. 2. Racism—Fiction. 3. Janitors—Fiction. 4. Interpersonal rela-
tions—Fiction. 5. Apartment buildings—Fiction. 6. Australia—Fiction.] I. Title.
PZ7.H59793Hav 2006   [Fic]—dc22   2005057157

Printed in the U.S.A.
2 4 6 8 10 9 7 5 3 1

Bloomsbury Publishing, Children's Books, U.S.A.
175 Fifth Avenue, New York, NY 10010

All papers used by Bloomsbury Publishing are natural, recyclable products
made from wood grown in well-managed forests. The manufacturing processes
conform to the environmental regulations of the country of origin.

For Alison

1

Hazel Green looked down from her balcony. It was early. Far below, the street was empty, and there was barely a sound.

The air was still chilly from the night. Hazel pulled her dressing gown snug around her. She put her hands on the railing. It was wet with dew. But Hazel didn't mind. She gripped the railing tight, just to feel the coldness of the metal. The sun was rising over the city. A bird twittered. Its voice was clear and pure. The bird warbled, stopped, and warbled again. Hazel listened. The chilly air made her skin tingle, and the chirping song of the bird made her smile, and the empty street made her happy, because everything she could see from her balcony on the twelfth floor, the whole city, was *hers*, and there wasn't anyone else to share it with.

Except, perhaps a bird. The bird sang again.

Suddenly a man appeared on the pavement below. He came out from a doorway, stopped, threw back his head, closed his eyes and turned his face up to feel the rays of the rising sun. He had a thick black moustache, just like a walrus, and so thick was it, and so black, that Hazel could see it clearly even from twelve floors above. Besides, it wasn't the first time she had seen it, and it wasn't the first time she had watched this particular man come out on the pavement and throw his head back and bask in the early sunlight, just like a big salty walrus stretching himself after a dip in the icy sea.

It was the baker, Mr Volio. When everyone else was just waking up, the bakers were almost at the end of their day. All through the night they worked, Mr Volio himself, and Andrew McAndrew, who kneaded the dough for the breads, and Martin, the pastrychef, and the two Mrs Volios—old Mrs Volio, who was Mr Volio's mother, and young Mrs Volio, his wife—who made the quiches and pies, and the four apprentices, who whipped the cream and oiled the trays and washed the tins and did all the other things that an apprentice has to do when learning to be a baker. And when morning came, after their work was done, they would finally sit down around the kneading table in the bakery to have a mug of cocoa, and only after *that* would Mr Volio go outside, to close his eyes and throw his head back and warm his face in the sunlight.

Hazel watched him. It was never possible to predict exactly how long Mr Volio would stand there like a walrus. Sometimes it was just a couple of seconds, and sometimes it might have been a couple of minutes. What did he think about while he had his eyes closed? A walrus would probably think about fish, Hazel decided. Or other walruses who were his friends. Or seals, perhaps, if he had just met one in the sea. But what if the walrus were really a person? That would make things quite a bit more complicated, thought Hazel, as she gazed down at Mr Volio, and wondered if anyone else had ever discovered such a walrus before . . .

Mr Volio opened his eyes. He looked up at Hazel's balcony. He grinned.

Hazel waved.

Mr Volio beckoned to her, gesturing with his hand in exactly the way a walrus would flap his flipper, Hazel thought, if he wanted someone to join him.

Hazel skipped down the stairs, all twelve flights of them. Waiting inside the bakery, she knew, would be the fresh products of the bakers' labour, baskets of breads, pallets of pies, quiches and crumbles, and most importantly, pastries, still warm from the ovens. Choosing which pastry to have was always the great dilemma. Chocolate Dippers, Cherry Flingers, Vanilla Slappers, Custard Clams . . . each of Mr Volio's inventions was more scrumptious than the one before, yet each was more delicious than the one that followed!

A Custard Clam, perhaps, thought Hazel, as she reached the bottom of the stairs. But did she *really* feel like a Custard Clam this morning? Perhaps it was the kind of morning for a Vanilla Slapper. Or an Apricot Custlet. Or a Chocolate Dipper. There was hardly a morning which wasn't the kind of morning for a Chocolate Dipper. In fact, Hazel couldn't remember a single one—

Hazel stopped. She was in the lobby of the apartment building. She had just heard a voice. But it wasn't Mr Volio's, and it wasn't coming from the street!

She listened for a moment. She heard the voice again. She crept across to the door that led from the lobby to the courtyard of the building. The door was ajar. Hazel peered through the crack.

There were two men in the courtyard. She could see who one of them was—Mr Egozian, the caretaker, dressed in his overalls. The other man was in his dressing gown and had his back towards Hazel. He was a big man, and was doing most of the talking. In fact, he wasn't talking. He was shouting.

'How many times do I have to tell you, Egozian?' he demanded harshly. 'Empty those rubbish bins quietly. You think you'll have a job here forever? You think I can't get rid of you? Wake me up one more time and you'll see what I'm talking about!'

'I'm always as quiet as I can be, Mr—'

'As quiet as you can be? Well, as quiet as you *can* be isn't good enough, then. I'm sick of your excuses. I'm sick of *you*, Egozian. How did you ever get this job, anyway? It was Mr Dunstan, wasn't it? Mr Dunstan used to protect you. Well, Dunstan's gone now. *I'm* the head of the Committee. You'd better get used to it.'

Mr Egozian didn't reply. Hazel could see the fear in his eyes.

The other man snorted. 'I've never liked you, Egozian. Look at you! I don't like *you* and I don't like your *kind*. Don't trust a single one of you. You're all the same. Liars, cheats . . .' The man paused. 'Just after what you can get, aren't you? Well, *watch out*, Egozian. Wake me up one more time, and that's it!'

The man turned.

There was no time to get out of the lobby. Hazel

jumped back and flattened herself against the wall behind the door. The door swung open and the man stormed straight past her. He marched off around the corner to the elevators without once looking back.

When he had gone, Hazel looked into the courtyard once more. It was empty. Mr Egozian had disappeared. Hazel went back through the lobby. She poked her head cautiously around the corner to see if the other man had already taken an elevator. There was no sign of him. By now, he was probably back in his apartment.

Hazel frowned. She knew who the other man was. As he came towards her from the courtyard, just as she jumped back behind the door, she had caught a glimpse of his face. Hazel shook her head in amazement. Of all people, what was *he* doing, shouting at Mr Egozian like that?

If she hadn't seen him for herself, heard the things he said with her own ears, Hazel would never have believed it.

2

'What would you like, Hazel?' said Mr Volio.

Hazel looked at the trays of pastries that stood against the wall. Chocolate Dippers, Vanilla Slappers, Cherry Flingers . . . they were all there.

'How about a Strawberry Comber?' said Mr Volio enticingly.

Hazel frowned.

'I know what she wants,' said young Mrs Volio. 'How about a lovely Chocolate Rollo, Hazel? What about that?'

Hazel shook her head. Something peculiar was happening to her. All these scrumptious pastries were on display . . . yet she didn't feel like eating any of them! This was *very* peculiar. In fact, she couldn't remember it happening before. But she had never come down the stairs to find someone shouting at Mr Egozian before, either.

'What is it, Hazel?' said old Mrs Volio. 'Is something wrong?'

'What could be wrong, Mama?' cried Mr Volio, and he thrust a lovely warm Strawberry Comber into Hazel's hand.

'Thank you, Mr Volio,' said Hazel, and she looked at it sitting on her palm.

'Well, aren't you going to eat it?' demanded the baker anxiously. There was nothing Mr Volio loved more than to see someone enjoying one of his pastries, and nothing that hurt him more than to see someone who took no pleasure in them.

Hazel nibbled at the Comber. She tasted its sweet, waffle-like base. Suddenly, she realised, everyone was watching her. She glanced around the bakery. Even the four apprentices, who were sitting in a row on the other side of the kneading table, were gazing at her solemnly. Usually they pretended to ignore her, only sneaking glances to pull a face.

'There *is* something wrong,' murmured Andrew McAndrew, folding his big, muscular arms across his chest.

'It's not the pastry, is it?' whispered Martin with dread.

Hazel shook her head. It wasn't the pastry. The Strawberry Comber was as good as ever, and she took another bite of it, to show him. Martin drew a sigh of relief.

'What is it, then?' said Mr Volio.

'I'm not certain,' said Hazel.

'Don't you have *any* idea?' asked the baker.

Any idea? Hazel always had ideas. But she wasn't always inclined to talk about them.

'Are you sick, Hazel?' said old Mrs Volio.

'Sick, Mama? Does she look sick? Does a girl who's sick get up at the crack of dawn and come to visit her favourite baker? Am I right, Hazel?'

Hazel nodded. Mr Volio was right.

'I know what's going on,' said the baker suddenly. 'Something's on your mind, isn't it, Hazel Green?'

Hazel nodded again. She took another bite of the Strawberry Comber. Something *was* on her mind.

. . .

The thing that was on Hazel's mind stayed there all day. More importantly, it got *inside* her mind as well. After school, Hazel went back to the courtyard. The courtyard was in the middle of the Moodey Building, as Hazel's apartment block was called, with rows and rows of windows on all four sides. Down here, it was as if you were at the bottom of an enormous well.

The courtyard was a good place to think. Hazel had often gone there before. Hardly anyone else ever appeared, so no one interrupted you to ask what you were thinking *about*. Mr Egozian, of course, would come to sweep up, and water the potplants that stood along the walls, but he never disturbed you. If he saw you were thinking, he'd sweep right around you and come back later to check there was nothing left where you had been sitting.

That was what Mr Egozian was like. He was always around, in the background, and never did anything to push himself forward. You were always seeing him here or there, doing one thing or another, but you never really paid attention to him.

Hazel sat down against one of the walls. This time, she hadn't come to think. It was Mr Egozian himself she was waiting for.

As she waited, she looked at the windows rising on the opposite side of the courtyard. Some of them had curtains and some were bare. Some had lights glowing and some were dark. It was funny how sometimes you couldn't see through windows at all, how they reflected things just as if they were mirrors. Hazel wondered why that was. They were just glass, after all. Hazel sighed. There was no point pretending she could work it out, because she couldn't. She didn't know enough about the Laws of Nature, as her friend the Yak called them. It was a shame that Nature had to have Laws. Laws weren't much fun. They were as bad as Rules, and Rules were as bad as Orders, which too many people, in Hazel Green's opinion, were fond of giving.

Hazel looked right up to the top of the building. Above the roof, big fluffy clouds were moving across the sky. They were moving fast. There must be quite a wind up there, Hazel thought, yet down here the air was perfectly still. In fact, no matter how windy it was above the building, there was hardly ever so much as a wisp of a breeze at the bottom of the courtyard. Why? It was all these Laws that Nature had! Without them, you'd never know what to expect. *That* would be much more interesting. One day you might come out to find the clouds in the sky barely moving at all while a terrific wind roared around your ears in the courtyard.

Hazel heard a door open. Mr Egozian appeared.

The caretaker was carrying a long-handled broom with a broad head. Clipped to its handle was a small brush and pan. A sack hung from his shoulder. He set directly to work, without disturbing her, just as he always did when he found Hazel sitting in the courtyard. He went to one corner, positioned his broom, and swept straight along the wall until he reached the opposite side.

Then he paused, unclipped his pan and brush from the broom handle, bent down, gathered the dust up in the pan, emptied it into his sack, clipped the brush and pan back on the handle and turned to push the broom across the courtyard again. He moved up and down systematically, pausing each time he reached the wall and swiftly repeating exactly the same set of actions.

Hazel watched him. Sometimes she wondered why he swept the courtyard so often. He did it every second day! She hardly swept her room every second week, and she *lived* there. No one lived in the courtyard. Hardly anyone even came out there. How much dust could there be? And dust doesn't just fall out of the sky, does it? Yet that didn't matter. Every second afternoon Mr Egozian came out to sweep, taking away every speck of dust in his sack.

Mr Egozian worked his way steadily to and fro across the courtyard. Soon he arrived beside Hazel, where he stopped and gathered up the dust with his brush and pan.

'Mr Egozian,' said Hazel.

Mr Egozian was just about to turn and move off again. He gripped the end of the broom handle and gazed at Hazel expectantly. He had soft brown eyes, and thick, wiry hair. It must have been black once, but now it was completely grey.

Hazel didn't know exactly what to say. Mr Egozian wasn't the kind of person to whom you talked very much. If you shouted Hello, you didn't expect an answer, because he was the kind of person who didn't speak very often, and usually just nodded in reply.

The *kind* of person? That was exactly the word Hazel had overheard that morning. His *kind*.

Mr Egozian was still watching, waiting for her to continue.

'I just wanted to say . . .' said Hazel, 'I just wanted to say I didn't hear you empty the rubbish bins this morning, Mr Egozian. I was up very early, and I didn't hear anything. And I would have, because it was very quiet then. Apart from the birds. But I still would have heard it, if you'd made a noise. I'm sure I would.'

Mr Egozian nodded. 'That's good,' he said. 'I'm glad I didn't disturb you.' He turned and began to push his broom again.

Mr Egozian obviously wasn't used to long conversations.

'Mr Egozian!' cried Hazel, running after him. 'I really mean what I said. I was up *very* early, and I didn't hear a thing. And I would have heard something if you'd made a noise. I've never heard you make a noise, and I'm often up early.'

Mr Egozian kept sweeping. They got to the other end of the courtyard and the caretaker knelt to gather up the dust.

'Why don't you empty the rubbish bins later in the day?' asked Hazel.

'I can't,' said Mr Egozian.

He was already pushing the broom again. Mr Egozian was a fast worker, thought Hazel, fast and silent. He probably had to be. The Moodey Building was a big place and there must be all kinds of things he had to do. If *she* had to sweep the courtyard, Hazel thought, looking around at the size of it, she could easily take a whole afternoon.

She ran to catch up with him again.

'Mr Egozian, why *can't* you empty the rubbish bins later in the day?'

'Because I have to do it early in the morning. I've been told.'

'Who told you?'

'The Committee. People have to be able to throw their rubbish down the chutes whenever they want, right until they go to bed. It would be inconvenient if they couldn't. So I have to wait until morning, and take the bins out to the alley before the rubbish collectors arrive.'

'I haven't heard that before.'

'It's a new rule,' said Mr Egozian. 'They made it after Mr Dunstan left.'

'But the rubbish collectors come very early, Mr Egozian. If people don't want to be disturbed, that's the *worst* time to empty the bins.'

The caretaker nodded.

'But that's ridiculous!' said Hazel. Rules were often ridiculous, and new rules were often more ridiculous than the rest. 'Why don't we just tell everyone to throw their rubbish out a bit earlier? Then you could move the bins, say, in the afternoon, and you wouldn't wake anyone up in the morning. Not that you ever *have* woken anyone up in the morning,' Hazel added hurriedly, 'but you *could*, if you dropped one of the bins . . .'

'I don't drop the bins,' said Mr Egozian quietly.

'Or if one of the lids fell off . . .'

'The lids don't fall off.'

'I know. I know they don't, Mr Egozian. At least, not this morning, because I would have heard. And I didn't hear anything, not a thing.'

Mr Egozian gazed at her. 'Is that what you came to tell me, Hazel? I'm very busy.'

Hazel frowned. She nodded.

It was *part* of what she had come to tell him. What the rest was, she wasn't sure, only she knew there must be something else, because she certainly didn't feel as if she had finished what she came to say.

'And I just wanted to say . . .' Hazel paused.

Mr Egozian kept watching her.

'I just wanted to say that I like you, Mr Egozian. Maybe certain other people don't like you, but I don't care. I don't care what anyone else says. And it doesn't matter whether Mr Dunstan's here or not, either! I still like you.'

Mr Egozian smiled. 'Thank you, Hazel,' he said after a moment. Then he turned and began pushing his broom again.

Hazel watched him. When he got to the wall, down he bent, sweeping up the dust and emptying it into his sack.

Suddenly it occurred to Hazel that Mr Egozian really had no reason to thank her. After all, she hadn't actually done anything for him.

3

'Well? What do you think?' said Mrs Gluck. She got up from her worktable, took a couple of steps back, and put her hands on her hips.

Hazel stepped back as well. So did Marcus Bunn. Marcus was a boy who wore spectacles with gold frames and had cheeks that were always shiny and red, as if he had just been out in the snow. He had come with Hazel to Mrs Gluck's flower shop to see the creation of the Tussleton Orchid Arrangement. Mrs Gluck said that this was going to be the largest, most complicated and most spectacular orchid arrangement she had ever made, which was saying a lot, considering that Mrs Gluck had been making flower arrangements for forty years, and orchid arrangements for at least twenty-seven of them. Obviously, Hazel wasn't going to miss it!

Neither was Marcus, although he would never have admitted that he liked coming with Hazel to visit the workroom at the back of the flower shop, which was no place for a *boy*. But for that matter, he probably wouldn't have admitted how much he liked Hazel Green, either, even though he liked her more than any other girl, more than anyone, in fact, and everybody knew it.

Now, after four solid hours of work, the Tussleton Orchid Arrangement stood before them. There must have been thirty different varieties of orchid, and not a single other type of flower. Long, curving stems rose gracefully amongst a tapestry of leaves, studded with flowers, yellow, white, mauve, pink, purple and orange. Some of the orchids combined two colours, some three. There were speckles, freckles and stripes. The tiniest of the orchids were as small as a bumblebee, and the largest would have spilled out of your hands. Yet each one was as delicate as a sculpture, with a trumpet-like centre and wing-like petals flaring around it.

Marcus stared.

Hazel walked around the table. From every side, the arrangement was bright, lush and complete.

'I wasn't sure about those large yellow ones,' said Mrs Gluck.

Hazel came around the table and stood beside Mrs Gluck.

'Those ones there, Hazel. Do you think they overpower the small pink ones just below? And those striped white ones?'

Hazel frowned. 'You could raise them a bit.'

Mrs Gluck nodded. 'Yes, I thought about that.' But she didn't touch the flowers. 'I think it's finished, though. What do you think? *Is* it finished?'

Mrs Gluck looked at Hazel. So did Marcus. Hazel considered the extraordinary arrangement on the table. Sometimes, according to Mrs Gluck, it took all of one's courage to *stop*. Not to add one last stem, or change one last thing, but just to stop, and accept that the work was finished. A true florist knew when that moment arrived. She might not be able to tell precisely how she knew it, but she *knew*. Something about the arrangement, perhaps the flowers themselves, said: 'Enough. We're ready.' In a way, it was easier to ignore that voice, to keep adding, changing, fiddling, until the last minute. But if you did, you would never regain the same balance and beauty again.

Hazel narrowed her eyes, concentrating. 'It's finished,' she said.

'How do you know?' whispered Marcus.

Hazel didn't reply. If a person had to ask that question, there was no point trying to explain.

Mrs Gluck nodded. She turned to Marcus. 'Do you see those purple ones?' she said. 'They come from India. And those ones there,' she said, pointing to a stem with small orange orchids, 'come from Brazil. And those ones come from Trinidad. Do you know where Trinidad is, Marcus?'

Marcus shook his head.

'No, I'm not sure myself. But they're so delicate they'll wilt before sunrise tomorrow. Just look at them.'

Marcus took a step closer to examine the orchids from Trinidad. The petals were white with flecks of crimson. The trumpet at the centre was crimson on the outside and deep yellow within.

'Do you know what it's called?' said Mrs Gluck.

Marcus shook his head.

'Eye of the Tiger.'

'Eye of the Tiger,' repeated Marcus, as if it really were a tiger, and not a flower, whose yellow eye was looking back at him.

'And it'll wilt before sunrise?' asked Hazel.

'That's right,' said Mrs Gluck.

Hazel shook her head. Why would someone want an arrangement with flowers that were going to last for only a few hours?

'Nothing's too good for the Tussletons,' said Mrs Gluck. 'When they sit down for their thirtieth wedding celebration tonight, everything has to be perfect. "Give me orchids, Mrs Gluck." That's what Mrs Tussleton said. "Give me something my guests will never forget." I've been planning this arrangement for a month. Do you know how tricky it is to make sure that orchids arrive from India, from Brazil, from Trinidad, and from seven other countries as well, all on the same day? But for the Tussletons, I had to do it. That's the kind of people they are. They want only the best of the best.'

Hazel frowned, still staring at the Eye of the Tiger. What was it that Mrs Gluck had just said? The *kind* of people the Tussletons are. There it was again, that word! The *kind* of people. The same word she had heard in the courtyard, two days before.

'What is it, Hazel?'

Hazel turned to Mrs Gluck. 'Is it good to be that kind of person?' she asked. 'Like the Tussletons?'

Mrs Gluck didn't answer straight away. 'Well, I don't think it's good *or* bad,' she said eventually. 'There are all kinds of people, Hazel. All kinds of people come into my shop.'

'All *kinds* of people?'

'Of course. I love meeting them. It's one of the best things about being a florist. Did I ever tell you about the truffleman who came into my shop one time? He spent

23

half the year searching for truffles, and the other half painting pictures.'

'Of truffles?' asked Marcus.

'I'm not sure,' said Mrs Gluck. 'I probably should have asked.'

'But you can't love meeting them all,' said Hazel. 'There must be some *kinds* of people you don't like.'

Mrs Gluck peered at Hazel closely. She sat down at her worktable before she answered.

'If you look hard enough,' she said at last, 'you can usually find something to like in everybody.'

'Yes, but what if you can't? What if there's a *kind* of person you don't like at all?'

'I don't think about people in that way,' said the florist.

'How do you think about them?'

'I don't think about them as kinds. I think each person's different.'

'But you said kinds! You said the Tussletons were a *kind* of person.'

Mrs Gluck looked at Marcus. Marcus nodded. His spectacles flashed in the light. 'You did, Mrs Gluck. You did say it.'

'Well, that was just an expression, Hazel. I don't think I really meant it.'

'So if you heard someone say "I don't like your kind", that would just be an expression as well, would it?'

'Who said that?' said Mrs Gluck quietly. 'Who did you hear?'

'I didn't say anyone said it, Mrs Gluck. I'm just saying *if* someone said it.'

Mrs Gluck thought. 'Well, I don't know if it would just be an expression. It might not be. It's possible. Someone might actually mean it.'

Hazel glanced at Marcus for a moment. He was watching her intently.

'What would you do if you heard someone say that, Mrs Gluck?' Hazel asked.

'What would I do?'

'Would you do anything?'

'Well, I don't think it's very nice. And I don't think it's right.'

'So what would you do? Or would you just ignore it?'

'Hazel, why don't you tell me what this is about?'

'I didn't say it was about anything.'

Mrs Gluck gazed at Hazel. Behind her, the magnificent Tussleton Orchid Arrangement stood on the table, lush, fresh, complete and ready to be delivered.

'Well, I don't know what I'd do,' said Mrs Gluck eventually. 'It's hard to say.'

'But you'd do something, wouldn't you?'

Mrs Gluck took a deep breath. She nodded. 'Yes. I probably would. I hope I would.'

Yes, thought Hazel. And just going along and telling someone you *did* like them wasn't enough. It didn't solve anything. It was the other person, the one who had made the comment in the first place, who was the problem.

'What was that about?' said Marcus, after they had left Mrs Gluck's shop.

Hazel didn't reply. You couldn't spend all your time explaining things to a boy who couldn't even hear the voice saying when an arrangement was finished.

'Didn't you hear the flowers speaking, Marcus?'

Marcus frowned. 'Were *they* the ones who said they didn't like a certain kind of person?'

'Perhaps,' said Hazel, just to see what Marcus would say next.

Marcus' eyes narrowed. 'Which ones? It was those little orange ones from Brazil, wasn't it? I bet it was!'

Hazel stopped. 'Marcus, *what* are you talking about?'

Marcus stopped as well. 'I'm not sure,' he said after a moment.

Hazel laughed. She started walking again. She didn't say anything else about the talking flowers, which was a relief for Marcus. It wasn't the first time he had found himself having a conversation with Hazel about something that seemed to make no sense at all. In fact, it wasn't even particularly unusual. And Marcus could never work out how it happened, because the conversations always seemed to start sensibly, and progress normally, yet they ended up ridiculously, with talking flowers or durgling buildings or something else that Marcus didn't even understand. And the strange thing was, the only conversations he ever had like that were the ones he had with Hazel Green!

They were walking along the pavement outside the Moodey Building. A little man came towards them, with a tiny chihuahua dog on the end of a leash. The chihuahua kept pulling at the leash, trying to get away. With the little man on one side, and the tiny dog on the other, and the leash stretching between them, they managed to take up almost the whole pavement. Hazel and Marcus split up to get around them, and met again on the other side.

The ground floor of the Moodey Building was occupied by all kinds of shops. Mrs Gluck's was only one of them. Hazel and Marcus were passing the Coughlins' fruit shop. Further along was the Frengels' delicatessen. A customer came out of the delicatessen and turned up the street with a package of delicacies under his arm.

'Have you heard the latest?' said Marcus suddenly. 'You'll never guess! There's going to be smoked salmon from Singapore. The Frengels are bringing it in specially.'

Hazel glanced at Marcus. 'They don't catch salmon in Singapore.'

'They do. I'm telling you, Hazel.'

'Wasn't it you who said the Frengels were bringing in grated coconut from Canada?'

'I never said that!' said Marcus. 'It was Hamish Rae.'

'You did say it, Marcus. I heard you.'

'Hamish said it first,' objected Marcus.

'And who told you they're getting smoked salmon from Singapore?'

'Hamish.'

Hazel shook her head. Marcus Bunn! He should just stop and listen to himself sometimes.

They had reached the delicatessen. They stopped at

the window. Jars of pickles and herrings were stacked behind the glass. At the counter, Mrs Frengel was slicing a salami for a customer.

'Have you heard about the chocolate?' whispered Marcus. 'There'll be chocolate from Belgium. They're getting that specially as well.'

'From Antwerp?' said Hazel.

Marcus glanced at her suspiciously, wondering whether this was going to turn into one of those conversations where the flowers started talking. 'Possibly,' he said.

'Are you *sure*?' said Hazel. Antwerp was the only name of a Belgian city that Hazel knew, apart from Brussels, and she was fairly certain that Marcus wouldn't know it at all.

'I'm not *absolutely* sure,' said Marcus eventually.

'You'd better find out then,' said Hazel.

'Yes,' said Marcus cautiously, 'I suppose I should.'

Hazel raised an eyebrow. They turned back to look inside the delicatessen. Mr Frengel was scooping olives into a container.

'Only three weeks to wait,' murmured Marcus, 'and then we'll get to taste everything.'

Hazel nodded. 'Let's hope they've started smoking those salmon in Singapore!'

4

The Frengels were the quietest, meekest shopkeepers you could imagine. They were small people. They both had fine, pale hair—so pale it was almost white—and light blue eyes, and the same shape of face, as well, with a flat forehead and square jaw. When their customers spoke, they listened attentively, and when they set about getting what their customers wanted—whether it was scooping up a cupful of olives, or filling a container with aubergine dip, or slicing a cheese on their razor-sharp slicer—they did it seriously, and never hastily, with a frown of concentration, as if it were the most important thing in the world. And at that moment perhaps it *was* the most important thing in the world, for the Frengels. When they were behind the counter they wore matching aprons with blue stripes, as if they had been *born* to be delicatessers.

It was twenty-five years since they had opened their delicatessen on the ground floor of the Moodey Building. To celebrate the occasion, they had decided to throw a party.

Of course, you don't necessarily need a reason to give a party, but if you do, a twenty-fifth anniversary is a very good one. On the other hand, some people, if they'd spent twenty-five years supplying delicacies to the Moodey Building, not to mention most of the other buildings in the neighbourhood, might have thought that everyone else should throw a party for *them*. But not the Frengels. If you wanted to find a delicatesser like that, you could go to Tegler's, which was two blocks away and where there was always noise and commotion. Old Joe Tegler virtually threw your packages at you when things got busy. If you ever complained he'd tell you to go away and not bother coming back. If you complained to one of the Frengels, they'd both spend sleepless nights, wondering what they'd done to upset you.

But the Frengels didn't make the decision to throw a party lightly, or quickly, or without a lot of discussion and consideration. What was it like to give a party? The two quiet, meek delicatessers had never done it before. They considered the idea for months. Perhaps, after all, they should settle for something less ambitious. Perhaps they should just send everybody a small present instead, a small container of anchovies, perhaps, with a selection of their finest black olives. No. Somehow that didn't seem enough. It wasn't the same as gathering everybody together like a big family and giving them the best food they'd ever tasted, with music and dancing to follow. Sending out containers of anchovies didn't compare. Besides, if you wanted to celebrate with your family, you didn't send them presents, did you? You brought them together.

That was the point. After twenty-five years, the Frengels felt as if virtually the entire Moodey Building was part of their family. They had seen children grow up in the building, and adults grow old. They had supplied the delicacies for parties to celebrate births, graduations, weddings, anniversaries and even for the gatherings that some people hold after funerals. No celebration in the Moodey Building would be complete without the spiced chicken wings, at least, that were the Frengels' speciality.

And everyone else agreed. As soon as word spread that the two delicatessers were thinking of giving a party, everyone immediately remembered how much of a family the Moodey Building really was, and how important a part the Frengels played within it. Quite simply, the Frengels' delicatessen was part of everyone's lives. There was hardly a single person who didn't go in there now and again, if not more often, to pick something up—except Mrs San Pietro di Marconi, who lived on the eighth floor and claimed she couldn't eat anything that was pickled, fried, jellied or spiced. Yet everyone knew she was secretly addicted to the Frengels' green olives steeped in chilli oil, and that she sent her grandson, Ralph, to get her half a dozen jars when he came to visit each week. If you ever talked to Mrs San Pietro di Marconi it wouldn't be two minutes before she was telling you how weak her stomach was, but anyone who could put away the Frengels' chillied olives at that rate must have had a stomach that was about as weak as an iron boot!

Where the Frengels got their delicacies, no one knew, and the Frengels never told. Once a year they'd both disappear for a few weeks, leaving the shop in the care of their assistants. But they weren't on holiday. After they came back, a whole new range of products would appear in the delicatessen, some of them not arriving for six months. If someone asked where a particular delicacy came from, the Frengels merely smiled politely and named a country, without telling *where* in that country they were talking about, or they'd reply even more vaguely, waving a hand in the air. They weren't being rude. It's the great secret of delicatessers, where they find their products, and you'll never meet one who'll reveal his sources. If a customer was foolish enough to ask old Joe Tegler a question like that, he'd throw their package across the counter and tell them they could try to find it for themselves next time. And he wouldn't serve them again until they'd apologised for being so nosy.

But Joe Tegler didn't go searching for new delights as often or as conscientiously as the Frengels. Nothing was too good for their big family of the Moodey Building. The dishes under the glass cover of their counter were crowded. From the roof hung a thick forest of salamis, and on the shelves rose wheels of cheeses in high, teetering stacks. Even the wall behind the counter was a display. It was tiled with wonderful hand-painted tiles, showing everything about food. One tile showed golden bundles of wheat, another had three herrings painted in blue. There was a ripe bunch of grapes, a pair of figs, a tree studded with yellow lemons, a lush red pomegranate . . . Other tiles showed the work that went into producing food and wine, a farmer gathering corn, a baker at his oven, a young man and woman treading grapes, fishermen hauling in nets, women churning butter . . . In short, the wall behind the Frengels' counter was like a book in itself, and it was well worth peering around the salamis and between the cheeses to read it.

The Frengels had bought the tiles from another delicatessen, which was about to be demolished. The tiles must have been a hundred years old. Each one had been carefully pried off the wall, cleaned and put up behind the Frengels' counter. The whole process had cost a fortune. But no one made tiles like that any more, and no matter how much they cost, no amount of money could replace them.

Once the idea of the Frengels' party was born, it rapidly began to grow. After all, the Frengels had never given a party before, so everyone had an opinion. Where should it be?. They should hire a hall. They should hire a park. They should hire a hall with a park. A park with a hall? A hall with a hill? A hill with a pond. What about the beach? What about the river? What about a boat *on* the river? What about—someone said—the courtyard?

The Frengels liked the idea of that. The courtyard, in the very centre of the Moodey Building. No place could be more appropriate. Some people grumbled, of course, especially the ones who wanted to go to the beach, but even they agreed eventually. Someone had a word with the Moodey Committee, which then invited the Frengels to apply to use the courtyard. The Frengels applied. Permission was granted.

But that was only the beginning! There was still so much to organise. The poor Frengels couldn't possibly manage it all by themselves, and Mrs Driscoll stepped in to help. No one was surprised at that. Mrs Driscoll was a famous organiser. She organised charity balls and council ceremonies and orchestral performances and anything else that people would let her organise, whether they paid her or not. She organised for the sheer love of organisation. She could organise a dog's birthday in a cattery, she was fond of saying, although people couldn't see why this would ever be required. Perhaps that was why she had never been invited to do it. The Frengels weren't sure whether they actually invited her to organise their party, either, but whether they invited her or not, she immediately accepted.

Soon the two striped delicatessers grew accustomed to the sight of Mrs Driscoll marching into their shop and calling them for a conference in the little room at the back where they did their accounts. No one else had ever been in that room before, except their assistants, and now Mrs Driscoll was there almost every day, showing them plans, informing them what she'd done or giving them orders. Mrs Driscoll gave a lot of orders, in fact, and not only to the Frengels. But whatever you thought about that, there was no doubt about one thing: she made things happen. When Mrs Driscoll decided something had to be done, it was done.

Bit by bit, Mrs Driscoll put all the pieces into place, just as if she were completing a jigsaw. She arranged for a huge banner that would be hung above the courtyard on the day of the party. She found people to supply tables and chairs. Crockery, glasses, knives and forks . . . she thought of everything. Mrs Gluck, of course, volunteered to provide the flower arrangements. Mr Breck, from the Vienna Café, agreed to supply waiters and waitresses. Mrs Driscoll found musicians. She found people to print the invitations, which she composed herself, naturally. She appointed seven of the Moodey children to deliver the invitations. Nothing was forgotten. She even found people to supply ice for the drinks.

'All you have to worry about,' Mrs Driscoll told the Frengels, 'is the food.'

The food! It was the most important day of the Frengels' lives. What amazing delicacies would they come up with? Soon the rumours started to fly. Ostrich eggs were on the menu, for sure, not to mention tender smoked goose and pickled Mexican artichokes stuffed with cheese. Someone heard there were going to be sweet milk cakes spiced with Indian chutneys. As the Moodey children walked to and from school each day, they discussed the party excitedly, exchanging the latest news about the Frengels' plans. Now, with three weeks to go, the rumours were getting wilder and wilder. Most of them were complete rubbish, as everyone knew. Hamish Rae, for a start, made up two new delicacies every day, and managed to convince himself that he had actually heard about at least one of them. Sometimes he managed to convince others, as well. There was the rumour about grated coconut from Canada, of course, which everyone believed until Abby Simpkin went home and checked in her encyclopaedia and found that there were no coconuts in Canada, which was much too cold for a tree like that, and there never had been any, at least not since some ancient time when the earth was warmer and Canadian dinosaurs munched coconuts for breakfast. Then there was the smoked salmon from Singapore, which Marcus mentioned to Hazel after they had left Mrs Gluck's flower shop. That was another of Hamish's inventions.

Hazel Green was looking forward to the Frengels' party as much as anybody, if not more. There were going to be all kinds of rare and exotic things to eat, she knew, from all over the world, which she might never have the chance to taste again. The foods that the Frengels were bringing in would be exotic enough without Hamish Rae's impossible concoctions!

Next day the latest scoop was bean curd stuffed with swallow tails, whatever that was meant to be. As they walked home from school, everyone was shouting about it.

'What do you think, Hazel Green?' cried Robert Fischer, bouncing around on the pavement.

'Swallow *tails*?' said Hazel derisively.

Robert Fischer glanced at Leon Davis, who always protected him. Leon folded his arms. 'Why not?' he said.

Hazel shrugged. 'You tell me,' she replied, and she kept walking.

'You tell *me*!' called Leon after her.

Hazel paused for a moment. It was a typical Leon Davis response. Normally, she would have turned around and *really* told him, just as he had asked, and straight to his face. Leon was her greatest rival, and lots of the Moodey children listened to him, almost as many as listened to Hazel herself. But it was the scene that she had witnessed in the courtyard, three mornings before, that was still the main thing on Hazel's mind. She still hadn't decided what to do about it. And for once, out of all the Davises, Leon wasn't the one Hazel was thinking about.

5

Telling Mr Egozian that she liked him wasn't enough. Hazel knew it even before she talked to Mrs Gluck. She had known it, in fact, as soon as she had said it to the caretaker. It was *something*, but it wasn't enough. Mr Egozian wasn't the problem. The problem, Hazel knew, was the other man who had shouted at him.

What she had heard that other man say, Hazel thought, was terrible. It was awful. The more she thought about it, the more awful it seemed. It wasn't the kind of thing you could just ignore. But what was she meant to do about it? It wasn't necessarily so easy to go up to an adult and tell him you thought he'd done an awful thing. And the man who had done it, whom she had heard shouting at the caretaker in the courtyard, was no ordinary adult. He was a big man with a booming voice. Everyone knew him. He was a powerful, important lawyer and Hazel had even seen his picture in the newspapers a few times.

Besides, even if you did have the courage just to walk up to an adult like that and tell him what you thought, it was quite likely that he'd just ignore you. Or laugh at you. Or think you weren't important enough even to *laugh* at. Adults could do things like that, Hazel knew, and she had seen it happen. It had even happened to her. There was the time, for instance, that old Mr Nevver left his hat on the table at the Vienna Café, where he always met his friends to drink coffee in the afternoon. Salomon, the waiter, found it and got on the telephone to tell Mr Nevver to come and collect it. So poor old Mr Nevver, who moved about as fast as a caterpillar, had to come all the way back down to the café, while it would have taken Salomon about two minutes to dash up to Mr Nevver's apartment and give it back to him. But when Hazel pointed this out, Salomon just laughed, and when she pointed this out to him again, he just laughed once more, and pushed her out of the café.

Of course, that was a long time ago, when Mr Nevver had been alive, and Hazel had been quite a bit younger. On the other hand, she wasn't all that much older, at least as far as an adult was concerned. And if Salomon had laughed at her, an important lawyer with a big, booming voice who sometimes had his picture in the newspapers probably wouldn't even bother to smile.

No, just going to tell him what she thought didn't seem like a good idea. And for that matter, why hadn't Mr Egozian said something when he had the chance? He'd just stood there and accepted it until the other man stormed away.

It was complicated. Maybe too complicated. What she needed, she thought, was some help from an expert in complicated things.

An expert in complicated things? Well, there was *one* person. The Yak. Maybe he wasn't exactly an expert, but he liked to think he was.

. . .

The problem with the Yak was that the complicated things in which he thought he was an expert were all mathematical, involving formulae and equations that could easily take up a whole page. His real name was Yakov Plonsk and he had a pointy face with a sharp chin. He and his parents had arrived a couple of years earlier from another country, Russia or Finland or Mozambique, no one knew for certain. They had taken the apartment on the third floor where old Mr Nevver used to live. And there the Yak stayed, coming out each day to walk to school by himself and walking home by himself as well, and hardly ever stopping to talk to anyone in the meantime . . . anyone, that is, except Hazel Green.

How it was that Hazel had become friends with the Yak was a long story, which went back all the way to the time Hazel had been accused of stealing the recipe for Mr Volio's Chocolate Dipper, not to mention the disappearance of Mr Petrusca's lobsters and the mysterious code-note that accompanied it. Both times, the Yak had helped her. Yet you could easily imagine that a boy like the Yak and a girl like Hazel would have very little in common. After all, the Yak was a mathematician, and spent all his time after school working on complicated problems like Fermat's Last Theorem, which, according to the Yak, was the greatest puzzle in mathematics. He also played the violin, because music, like mathematics, has order. If there was one word to summarise what went on in the Yak's mind, that was it. Order. But if there was one thing to summarise what went on in Hazel Green's mind, it was disorder. Or better yet, *chaos*!

Yet they *were* friends. At least, Hazel thought they were. It wasn't necessarily so easy to be sure, because the Yak wasn't like any other friend Hazel had ever had. They didn't really *do* things together, for example. Most of the time, they just talked. But he certainly wasn't one of her enemies! In other words, he was the Yak, and there was no point looking for any other way to describe him.

And then there was the Yak's mother. She wasn't like any other mother Hazel had ever seen. She was slim and tall and always dressed in elegant clothes. Her hair, which swirled around and behind and above her head like a seashell, made her look even taller. In other words, she was the Yak's mother, and there was no other way to describe her, either.

The Yak's mother opened the door. She was wearing a silk gown the colour of lavender, and her fingernails were painted lavender as well. Her shoes were grey. Her hair was sandy with honey-coloured streaks. And she was holding a pair of eyeglasses with thin gold frames.

'Are you here to see Yakov?' said the Yak's mother.

Hazel nodded. The Yak's mother liked to ask this question when she came to the door, even though Hazel always gave the same answer. Perhaps she was waiting for the day when Hazel would say she had come to see someone else.

The Yak's mother held out her glasses towards Hazel. 'I've decided to try spectacles,' she said.

'Why?' said Hazel. 'Can't you see?'

The Yak's mother gave Hazel a surprised glance. Then she put the spectacles on her nose. 'What do you think?'

Hazel wasn't sure she thought *anything* yet.

After a moment the Yak's mother nodded. She took the glasses off and gazed at them. 'That's what I was wondering as well.' She sighed. 'But I might keep them. You never know.'

Hazel nodded. That's right, you *never* knew.

'Go into the front room,' said the Yak's mother. 'I'll get Yakov.'

The Yak's mother disappeared. The apartment was full of furniture, and new things were always being added, even though you wouldn't imagine there was room for a single extra piece. In the hallway alone there was a lamp, a table, a coat stand, a small desk, a set of bookshelves, two chairs, a shoe rack, a porcelain vase, a potted plant, a magazine holder, a grandfather clock, an enormous urn for umbrellas, a pair of silver candlesticks and a wooden box with carved scenery on the sides, not to mention the oil paintings on the walls and the Persian rug on the floor. The front room was full of sofas and armchairs. Hazel sat down on a green sofa that stood back to back with another, in blue and yellow, where she sometimes sat instead. A few minutes later the Yak arrived.

'Hello,' said the Yak.

'Hello,' said Hazel, and she smiled broadly, and glanced at the Yak's mother, who was standing in the doorway.

The Yak's mother smiled back at her.

'Your mother's trying spectacles, Yakov,' whispered Hazel after the Yak had sat down and his mother had gone.

'Is she?'

'Haven't you noticed?'

The Yak shook his head.

Hazel wasn't surprised. For the Yak to notice something, it had to come with a plus sign or a minus sign or, best of all, an equals sign. According to the Yak, the equals sign was the king of signs, because it indicated balance, and balance indicated harmony, and harmony, of course, indicated *order*.

'Well, I'm just telling you,' said Hazel. 'I thought you'd want to know.'

'Thank you,' said the Yak. He began to think. 'Why would do I want to know?'

Hazel raised an eyebrow. For someone who spent his time solving complicated problems, there were a lot of surprisingly simple things the Yak didn't understand.

The Yak was deep in thought. Hazel gazed at him. Who knew what he was thinking about now? Not his mother's spectacles! It took the Yak only a minute to start thinking about one of his mathematical problems, and five minutes for him to start thinking about five of them. And besides, he could also play the violin in his head, and if you let him start he wouldn't stop until he had finished the piece.

'Yakov!'

The Yak looked up.

'I've got a problem for you.'

'What is it?' said the Yak, sitting forward eagerly. The Yak hardly ever went out of his apartment, except to go to school, but he loved hearing from Hazel about the knotty problems people were struggling with in their lives, so he could sit there on the sofa and unknot them without leaving his front room. He probably wouldn't even go to the Frengels' party, for instance, but he'd want to hear all about it from Hazel. 'Don't tell me, it's the Rosellis' grandson again! They want him to go into the family business, I know, and he wants to be a jeweller. How can they expect him to change, Hazel? How? Jewellery's an art. Think about rings. A ring has symmetry, harmony, balance . . .'

'Order?'

'Exactly. How can they expect him to be happy making pasta?'

'Doesn't pasta have order?' demanded Hazel, although she had never thought about pasta as being particularly orderly before. 'What about those little round ones? They have as much symmetry as a ring. They *are* rings!'

The Yak frowned. 'That's true,' he said.

Hazel smiled to herself. That was one of the strangest things about the Yak. He always saw when someone else was right, even if it went directly against what he was saying, and he always admitted it as well! Hardly any of the other Moodey kids did that. They'd argue, shout, call each other names or even start punching each other, all to avoid admitting they were wrong. Hazel herself knew all the tricks, and was quite skilled in using them. After all, what was the point in admitting you were wrong, on one occasion or another, if the people around you would never admit the same thing when they were the ones who were mistaken?

That was one of the reasons it was so interesting talking with the Yak, to see how often you could get him to admit that he needed to reconsider.

'It's complicated,' said the Yak. 'You eat pasta, but you don't eat jewellery. So you could say that the first sort of order disappears when you eat it, but the other sort remains.'

'But order's eternal . . . and universal . . .' said Hazel, trying to remember all the things the Yak was always saying about it. Of course most of it was nonsense, in her opinion, but occasionally you had to humour a boy like the Yak, or he'd go off playing the violin in his head again. 'You can't *eat* it. You can eat pasta, Yakov, but you can't eat order.'

The Yak frowned. 'That's an interesting point,' he said. 'I need to think about that.'

'No!' cried Hazel in dismay. 'Don't start thinking, Yakov. Don't!'

The Yak scowled. 'I don't see why you came here to ask my opinion about the Rosellis' grandson if you don't want me to give it any thought.'

'That's exactly where you're mistaken, Yakov Plonsk.'

'You do want me to give it some thought?'

'No. I didn't come here to ask you about the Rosellis' grandson. It's got nothing to do with him.'

'Who's it got to do with?'

'Me.'

6

The Yak peered at Hazel suspiciously. So, she had come to tell him about something that involved her. For the Yak, that was the first sign of danger. Whenever Hazel came to talk to him about something that involved *her*, it always seemed to end up involving *him*, and he never seemed to be able to prevent it. The second sign of danger, he knew, was if she said that he wouldn't have to do anything, she just wanted to hear what he thought.

'You won't have to *do* anything,' said Hazel, 'I just want to hear what you think.'

The Yak shook his head.

'Really, Yakov.'

'Hazel . . .'

'Anyway,' said Hazel, 'it's not really about me. It's actually about Mr Egozian.'

The Yak sighed. 'Who's Mr Egozian?' he asked reluctantly.

'*Who's Mr Egozian?* Yakov, you'll be asking where Antwerp is next!'

'No I won't. I know where Antwerp is: Belgium.'

'Do you know if they make chocolates there?'

The Yak frowned. 'Chocolates?'

'You see! You'll be asking about that next, as well. Now listen, Mr Egozian is the caretaker here in the Moodey Building, and if you don't know him already you should go and introduce yourself.'

'Now?' said the Yak.

'Very funny, Yakov.'

The Yak grinned. His whole pointy face scrunched up.

Hazel sighed. She settled back in the green sofa with her arms crossed and waited for the Yak to be serious again. Mathematicians were very strange creatures, to judge from the Yak, and found nothing so funny as the jokes they made themselves. But a lot of people were like that, thought Hazel, not only mathematicians.

'Now, are you listening, Yakov?'

The Yak nodded. He nodded a bit extravagantly, thought Hazel, so she fixed him with a stern stare, and waited a moment longer, so he'd realise this wasn't a time to make extravagant gestures or amuse himself with his so-called jokes.

'I'm going to say something to you, Yakov. Are you ready? Here it is: I don't like your kind of people!'

The Yak didn't reply. He didn't even blink.

'Well?' said Hazel.

Suddenly the Yak's face scrunched up. But it didn't scrunch the way it scrunched when he grinned. It scrunched in a kind of hurt, painful way.

'Why do you have to say that?' he whispered. 'You're the only one I ever let in here . . .'

'I'm the only one who ever comes here.'

'Why do you have to say that, then? If you don't like me, you don't have to come. Did I ever ask you to come? Did I ever ask you—'

'Yakov! I don't *mean* it. How could you think that? I'm only repeating what I heard.'

'You heard it? So you've got to repeat it?' The Yak shook his head, still looking at Hazel with a pained glance. 'Do you think it's the first time *I've* heard it? Do you know what it's like to come from a different country, Hazel Green? Do you know the things people say to you when you first arrive, when you're learning a new language? Maybe you should think about *that*. No, I'll make it easy for you. Let me tell you. The first person who said he didn't like my kind of people was a taxi driver. Actually, he didn't say it to me, he said it to my mother. At least we think that's what he said. We weren't sure, because we couldn't understand him properly. This would have been about . . . oh . . . about three hours after we arrived. And then . . .'

Hazel listened. She kept meaning to interrupt, to tell the Yak that what she had heard wasn't about him, or *his* kind of people, but every time she opened her mouth to speak, he told her about some other person who had made a similar remark. His face was red, his body was trembling, and his voice shook in a way that Hazel had never heard from him before.

The Yak's mother appeared in the doorway.

'It's all right, Mrs Plonsk,' said Hazel.

The Yak looked around.

'Yakov?' said the Yak's mother.

The Yak drew a deep breath. Then he nodded.

The Yak's mother stayed a moment longer, looking at them uncertainly. Finally she went away again.

'Do you want me to continue?' said the Yak.

Hazel shook her head. 'I didn't realise,' she murmured.

'Of course you didn't. Why should you? You've never been in that situation. You've always been a local, never a foreigner. You've never been *different*, have you?'

Hazel frowned. She wouldn't exactly say she'd never been *different*. There were all kinds of *different*. Everyone was *different*, when you thought about it hard enough. But maybe the Yak was talking about a different kind of different, if that was possible.

'So what do you do?' asked Hazel eventually.

The Yak looked at her blankly.

'What do you do? You don't just let them say those things, do you?'

The Yak shook his head bitterly. 'What would you suggest, Hazel Green?'

Hazel stared at him in disbelief. He *did* just let people say those things.

'I wish I could show them,' muttered the Yak, staring at the carpet. 'They should be ashamed of themselves. I wish I could just make them *feel* what it's like.'

'How?'

The Yak shrugged hopelessly, still gazing at the floor. Hazel watched him.

'Yakov?'

The Yak looked up.

'You know when I said "I don't like your kind of people"? Well, it wasn't meant for you.'

'I know. You told me, you just happened to hear it. Thanks for letting me know.'

'No. I mean, it wasn't about you at all. The person I heard, he wasn't talking about you or your people.'

Yakov sat back in his chair. 'Who was he talking about?' he asked quietly.

'Mr Egozian.'

'Mr Egozian?' demanded the Yak. 'The caretaker you told me about? You expect me to believe that?'

'Why not?' demanded Hazel. 'Do you think you're the only one who's important enough for people to dislike?'

The Yak nodded. 'You're right. I'm sorry.' He paused for a moment. 'Did he hear it, this Mr Egozian.'

Hazel nodded.

'What did he do?'

'Nothing,' said Hazel.

'Nothing? He just accepted it?'

'He just accepted it,' said Hazel.

The Yak winced. 'Who said it to him?'

'I shouldn't tell you,' said Hazel.

'Then you shouldn't have told me anything!' retorted the Yak. 'Who was it?'

'You'll never believe it.'

'Hazel . . .'

Hazel took a deep breath. 'It was Mr Davis.'

'You don't mean Leon's father?'

Hazel nodded. 'That's *exactly* who I mean.'

'You said it yourself,' said Hazel, when she had finished telling the Yak what Mr Davis had said in the courtyard, 'we have to show him.'

'I didn't say we have to show him,' replied the Yak, slowly and carefully. 'First of all, I didn't say *we*. Second,

I said I wanted to show people what it's like, I didn't say I *had* to show them. And third, I didn't say *him*. I certainly didn't tell you to go and show someone like Mr Davis.'

'It's the same thing,' muttered Hazel.

'It's not the same thing. I was talking about Principle. You're talking about Practice. Principle and Practice are quite different,' declared the Yak, as if he were giving some kind of lesson. The Yak was always a lot happier talking about ideas than actually doing anything based on those ideas. 'Principle has practices, and Practice has principles,' he was saying. 'Listen carefully and I'll explain . . .'

Hazel listened carefully for about a second. She didn't want to hear why Principle and Practice were different. If you listened long enough to a mathematician, you'd never *do* anything. She gazed at the window. She remembered that she'd meant to ask the Yak about the Laws of Nature and why you could see into some windows and not into others when you were sitting in the courtyard. But that would have to wait. Not because the Yak was still talking—which he was—but because Hazel was getting an idea.

It was a very interesting idea. Hazel considered it as it grew and formed in her mind. Fortunately, the Yak seemed to have a lot to say about the difference between Principle and Practice, so he was able to entertain himself while she thought about it. The more she considered the idea, the better it seemed. There was only one problem: it would take *two* people to make it work. But that wasn't a problem she couldn't overcome . . . with a little bit of help . . .

'Yakov,' she said suddenly, 'that's enough!'

The Yak stopped in surprise. He was barely halfway through the practices of Principle, and he hadn't even started on the principles of Practice.

'We have to show Mr Davis. We just *have* to!'

'No,' said the Yak cautiously, 'you obviously haven't been listening. It would be good if we *could* show him . . .'

'Exactly. And I've worked out a way.'

'Have you?' said the Yak, not really wanting to hear the answer.

'Yes. You said we have to make him feel ashamed. Well, I know how we can do it!'

The Yak sighed. 'We?'

'What do you think? I can't do it by myself. Yakov,' announced Hazel, 'this is your lucky day! I've got a plan that's perfect, and I'm giving *you* the chance to help me.'

The Yak stared in disbelief. She was giving him the chance to help her? And had he asked for such a chance? How did it happen that you said one thing to Hazel Green, and she always managed to hear another?

'Of course, there'd be lots of other people who'd want this chance,' said Hazel, 'but I'm giving it to *you*, Yakov Plonsk, and I'll tell you why. You deserve it. You've been in that situation, the foreigner, not the local. You know what it is to suffer because people think you're different. So if someone is making other people suffer because *they're* different, you'd obviously want to help punish him.' Hazel paused. 'Don't thank me,' she added graciously, 'I'm just pleased you'll have the opportunity.'

'It doesn't follow that I *want* the opportunity,' said the Yak, holding up a finger. 'Just because I know what it's like to be different, it doesn't follow, from that premise, that I should care when someone else suffers because of it.'

'It doesn't follow from that premise?' Hazel said slowly, and peered at the Yak as if she were giving him the time to give her a *serious* answer. 'All right,' she said eventually, as if his time was up, 'you don't care. Fine. Just do one more thing for me, Yakov, and then I'll leave you alone. Swear that you don't care. Swear on your nose.'

The Yak didn't reply.

'Go ahead. Swear you don't care when a person tells someone else he doesn't like his kind of people. On your nose, if you wouldn't mind.'

The Yak grimaced. 'That's ridiculous!' he muttered.

Of course it was ridiculous, that was the whole point. To swear on your nose, for the Moodey children, was the biggest test, the most solemn oath, and no one would dare to misuse it.

'Go on,' said Hazel.

The Yak put his finger on his nose. Hazel waited for him to speak, watching him mercilessly with her fiercest, most penetrating gaze. It almost hurt to gaze at someone like that—she could barely imagine what it must be like on the receiving end!

The Yak took his finger away.

Hazel smiled. 'You see. You can't swear, can you? You *do* care.'

The Yak shook his head. Hazel Green had done it again!

7

The plan was all worked out. Every detail was clear in Hazel's mind. After a couple of days of investigation—by which Hazel meant hanging around the lobby—she had discovered that Mr Davis always arrived home at exactly the same time each night. Or almost exactly the same time, between 7.02 and 7.06 in the evening. This evening, by 7.10 at the latest, he'd be feeling so ashamed of himself he'd wish the ground would just open up and swallow him!

The precision of the timing pleased the Yak. It appealed to his sense of mathematical accuracy. But that was about the only thing that did.

'Nothing can go wrong. I'm telling you. *Nothing* can go wrong,' Hazel assured him, when she met the Yak, as arranged, outside his apartment at 6.55 on Thursday evening.

'*Nothing* can go wrong? I've thought of fourteen things that could go wrong. *First*, Mr Davis might not hear you. *Second*, someone else might interfere before he gets close enough to do anything. *Third . . .*'

Hazel walked to the elevator. She pressed the button.

'. . . *Fifth*, you might forget what you have to say . . .'

The elevator doors opened. Hazel got in and pressed the button for the ground floor.

'. . . *Eighth*, Mr Davis might be distracted after he hears you . . .'

'Yakov, why don't you just concentrate on what *you* have to do so you don't mess it up?'

'Because I'm only up to number nine. And the risk of me messing it up is number fourteen!'

Hazel sighed. The doors opened at the ground floor. They got out of the elevator, and Mrs Nimsky and her cousin got in. No one liked Mrs Nimsky's cousin—except Mrs Nimsky's aunt, of course—because he gambled too much and used other people's scissors without returning them. He was a great borrower of scissors, but by now no one in the Moodey Building would lend him a pair.

'Now remember,' whispered Hazel, as the doors closed behind Mrs Nimsky and her cousin, 'just stand there. Look sad. Try to argue back, if you like. Do whatever comes naturally and leave the rest to me. If you want to cry, cry.'

'I don't want to cry.'

'You might. All I'm saying is, a couple of tears would be helpful. Think of something sad. Imagine someone already solved Fermat's Last Theorem.'

'That's not funny, Hazel.'

'Exactly. You see, think of that. Fermat's Last Theorem. Solved, finished, sorted. Go on, Yakov, if you can cry, cry. That'll *really* show Mr Davis.'

Hazel glanced around the lobby. They were alone. She looked at the clock on the wall above the elevators. Seven o'clock, exactly. She could hear the chimes of another clock coming faintly from somewhere else.

'Come and stand over here, where he can't miss us.'

They walked further into the lobby.

'Let's pretend we're talking while we wait.'

'That'd be the first time you had to *pretend* you were talking, Hazel Green.'

Hazel grinned. The Yak was showing some fight. Excellent!

'I wouldn't have to talk so much if *you* ever had anything sensible to say,' retorted Hazel.

The Yak looked at her in confusion. Was she serious or had she already begun to play her part?

Someone came out of one of the elevators and walked past them.

'I think I say some very sensible things,' murmured the Yak when they were alone again.

'Oh, that's what you think, is it?' said Hazel, glancing at the clock once more. 'And have you ever met anyone else who thinks so? Let me know who they are. I'd *really* like to meet them.'

The Yak stared.

'Names, Yak!' she demanded, turning on him. 'Let's have some names! If you've got any friends, they must have names. Let's have them. Names, Yak! Names, Yak!'

The Yak's face was going red. His lip was trembling.

Hazel heard someone behind her. She glanced around. Mr Davis had just walked into the lobby, carrying his briefcase.

'Perfect, Yakov. Just keep doing exactly what you're doing now,' she whispered. Then she shouted again. 'You think you're so smart! Think you know all the answers. Well, I'll tell you something, Yakov Plonsk. I don't like you. Never have. I don't like you and I don't like your *kind of people.*'

The Yak was staring at her in dismay.

'Say something,' whispered Hazel.

But the Yak just stared. Now Hazel could see a tear starting up at the corner of each of his eyes. Excellent!

'Did you hear me?' she shouted at the top of her voice. 'I don't *like* your *kind of*—'

Hazel stopped. Mr Davis was standing over her, with his hand on his hip and an angry look on his face.

Hazel had to bite her lips to keep from smiling. Everything was going perfectly. What a plan, if she did say so herself!

'Children,' boomed Mr Davis, 'if you want to fight, go outside.'

Hazel frowned. Excuse me? What was that she just heard? Go outside? Go outside if you want to fight? Is that all Mr Davis had to say?

'Go on! Out you go! We won't have fighting in here!'

The Yak had already started walking.

Mr Davis was glaring at her, ordering her out.

Hazel desperately tried to think. No, this wasn't in the plan. It was all going wrong, terribly wrong. Mr Davis wasn't meant to tell her to go outside. He was meant to give her a lecture about what an awful thing she had said, as any normal adult would. And once he had given his lecture—which he would give in a very self-righteous and superior tone, as adults do—she was going to tell him that she was only repeating what *he* had said to Mr Egozian. And if it was wrong for her, then it must be wrong for *him*. And if he lectured her, then he ought to lecture *himself*. And then she would walk away and leave him feeling foolish, nasty and ashamed, just wishing the ground would open up and swallow him.

'Out!' boomed Mr Davis, in a voice that sounded anything but ashamed.

'But . . .' stammered Hazel.

'You heard me!'

'But . . .'

'Out! If you want to fight, fight outside!'

Outside, the Yak was waiting.

'What did you mean by that?' he said. '*If* I had any friends? You're my friend, aren't you?'

'What?' said Hazel. She looked back into the lobby. The elevator doors were closed, and Mr Davis had already disappeared, as if the whole episode didn't warrant another moment of his time. Why had she gone outside when Mr Davis told her? Why hadn't she tried to say something else? It was as if her feet took her out by themselves, while her mind had still been trying to understand what was happening.

'Did you mean those things?'

'What things?' said Hazel.

'All the things you said.'

Hazel could hardly remember a word she had uttered. 'Yakov, you know why I said them.' Hazel frowned. 'It was just to show Mr Davis. It wasn't serious.'

'Well, you showed him, Hazel! He looked *really* ashamed.'

'Very funny, Yakov.' Hazel shook her head. She still

couldn't believe it. It was a perfect plan—but it hadn't worked. 'Did *you* think of that?' she said suddenly. 'Was it one of the fourteen things on your list?'

'That Mr Davis wouldn't give you your lecture?'

'That he wouldn't even care what I was saying? That all he'd care about was getting us out of the building?'

The Yak shook his head. 'No, it wasn't.'

'No,' said Hazel. 'I never thought of it either. It was the one thing that didn't cross my mind.'

'Hazel, lots of things didn't cross your mind.'

It was true, lots of things *hadn't* crossed Hazel's mind. And there was one more thing that still hadn't crossed it: that someone else might have been in the lobby, someone who came in just after Mr Davis and slipped quietly across to the corner, where she stood and watched everything that happened.

8

The lady who saw Hazel Green's fight with the Yak was called Mrs Burston. She had come in a few seconds after Mr Davis, just in time to hear the things that Hazel Green was shouting at the boy right there in the middle of the lobby, and to see Mr Davis order them out of the building. In all the hubbub, no one noticed her as she watched from the corner. The two children went out of the lobby in one direction, Mr Davis went to the elevators in the other direction, and Mrs Burston was left all by herself. For a moment she just stood there, thinking about what she had seen. She couldn't believe it. The things that Hazel Green had said! It was all so awful. It was so horrible. It was so . . . *delicious*.

Then she crossed the lobby and pressed the elevator button with a strange smile on her lips.

Mrs Burston went up to her apartment. She lived on the seventh floor, with a parrot. The parrot had a cage but Mrs Burston sometimes let it fly free in her apartment for hours at a time. It wasn't the first parrot she had had. Mrs Burston had lived in the Moodey Building for years, and during that time a number of parrots had come and gone in her apartment, one after the other. Whenever one died she replaced it with a bird of almost identical appearance, so no one knew *precisely* when a new one arrived. Yet no parrot could live for as long as Mrs Burston had lived in the Moodey Building, or even for half as long, so it must have happened a number of times. And she called them all by the same name, Manfred.

Mrs Burston liked to talk to Manfred. The bird would watch her with a beady, eager eye. If he was inclined to fly around too much, Mrs Burston would put him in his cage, so he would be sure to listen. Sometimes Manfred even repeated a word or two of whatever it was Mrs Burston had been telling him. And Mrs Burston told him everything. Each evening, Manfred got a complete summary of all the things his owner had seen and heard during the course of the day. In short, Manfred was a well-informed bird, certainly the most knowledgeable parrot in the Moodey Building, if not the whole city.

But the truth was, Manfred was only Mrs Burston's rehearsal audience. Fortunately, being a parrot, he probably didn't realise this. When she came home each evening and told Manfred everything she had seen and heard, Mrs Burston was really listening to herself, trying to work out how she sounded and whether she could improve the effect. Sometimes she would say the same thing to Manfred three, four or five times over, trying out different versions of a particular story and perfecting her delivery. And sometimes she imagined that the parrot's eye became a little brighter, his beak a little higher, when she tried out one particular way of saying something, which she regarded as an encouraging sign. When he actually repeated a word, in his croaky bird-voice, it was the most positive sign of all!

But even if Manfred listened to Mrs Burston's news, and sometimes repeated a word or two, the parrot could never give her any fresh information in return. And news, as everybody knows, is a powerful currency, which many people like to trade. Mrs Burston was a great trader of news. She enjoyed nothing more than finding someone who was eager to hear her information, and who had information of their own to tell her in exchange. Once she had rehearsed with Manfred each evening, Mrs Burston was ready to set to work.

She didn't go to a market for this, or to a shop, or even necessarily out of her own apartment. The trade in news isn't like selling fish or buying watermelons. All you need is a telephone, as long as there's someone on the other end, or a cup of tea with some friends who are enthusiastic news traders as well. Mrs Burston had a lot of friends like that. If she had a really interesting piece of news, she might easily talk to half a dozen people in a single evening, and soon enough each of them would have spoken to another half-dozen in their turn.

That Thursday evening, she knew, she was going to be busy!

'Guess who I saw,' she said to Manfred as soon as she had closed the door of her apartment behind her. 'Hazel Green with that strange boy, Yakov whatever-his-name-is. And guess what she said . . .'

No, that wasn't very original.

'Who's the *last* person you'd expect to hear saying that she didn't . . .'

No, that was too long and clumsy. People would lose track of what she was saying before she'd finished saying it. Mrs Burston had learned that short sentences were always better, particularly at the start of a story.

'Did you hear Hazel Green in the lobby today? She said the most horrible thing I've ever heard. Horrible!'

Manfred cocked his head. His eye brightened. '*Holible . . . Holible . . .*' he croaked.

'Yes, Manfred. The most *horrible* thing. I'm almost too ashamed to say it. Listen, I'll tell you what it was . . .'

Soon, Mrs Burston was ready. She made the first of her phone calls. By the end of the evening, the news had spread via the phone line out of her apartment in half a dozen different directions. And already it was spreading again, on the phone lines from all the people Mrs Burston had just told. And then it spread again. And each time it spread, it became worse. The things Hazel was supposed to have said were more and more revolting. The things she was supposed to have done became more and more malicious. Eventually she was supposed to have tried to strangle the boy, and only the quick intervention of Mr Davis had saved his life. And the peculiar thing was that when this version of the incident eventually made its way back to Mrs Burston, she didn't say anything to correct it, and was soon repeating it herself.

By morning, half the Moodey Building knew, or *thought* they knew, what Hazel had done the evening before.

But Hazel Green, in her room on the twelfth floor, was unaware that anything was happening. When she stepped out of her apartment the next morning, she had no idea how the world had changed overnight.

9

The next morning, as the Moodey children walked to school, there was a lot of whispering. For the past few days, the main topic of conversation had been the Frengels' foods, and which of Hamish Rae's rumours, if any, were true. But there wasn't any talk about the Frengels today. Instead, there were a lot of sideways glances and hushed words from people who seemed to know something, and a lot of surprised stares from people who didn't. And Hazel soon noticed that the sideways glances and surprised stares all seemed to be directed at her.

Hazel looked around. People were bunched together, heads were close, eyes looked at her, looked away, looked back again. What was going on? Suddenly Robert Fischer starting jumping around on the pavement, shouting at the top of his lungs.

'*Hazel hates the Ya-ak! Hazel hates the Ya-ak!*'

Robert's satchel bobbed around as he jumped. If he jumped high enough, it might hit him in the back of the head.

'Hazel hates the— *Ow!*' cried Robert.

Hazel laughed.

Everyone else had stopped. Now that Robert Fischer had brought the whispering to an end, they wanted to know the truth. Only Robert himself was still going, bouncing down the pavement ahead of them.

They weren't even halfway to school. On the other side of the road, the children from the Crabstree Building were passing by, glancing over at them to see why they had stopped. Suddenly one of them shouted. 'Don't be late, Moodeys. Dumb kids need all the lessons they can get!'

The Moodey kids turned. When the Moodey Building was challenged, arguments were set aside! With one voice, they shouted across the road.

Crabstreeters all are cheaters,
One's called John, the rest are Peters!

The Crabstreeters immediately retorted:

Look at the kids, the kids from Moodey!
Their Dad's called Jim, their Mum's called Trudi!

These were the usual taunts. No one knew who had first invented them, or why, or what was wrong with being called John, or Jim, or Peter, or even Trudi, for that matter. Besides, no one's mother in the Moodey Building was called Trudi, as far as anyone knew. A few adults on the pavement stopped to watch, but most hurried past, shaking their heads or clicking their tongues in disapproval of these *unruly* children who were shouting at each other across the street. The Moodeys called out:

Crabs, Crabs, Here come the Crabbers,
They're the world's biggest Blabbers!

To which the Crabstreeters began to respond:

Moodey, Moodey kids are dumb,
We'll kick them all up . . .

But the chant died out before it reached the end, as some of the older Crabstreeters looked at their watches, realised they were going to be late, and began to pull the younger ones along. The Moodeys laughed and jeered and pulled faces at them. When the Crabstreeters had gone, they got back to business.

'Well?' said Leon Davis.

'Well, what?' said Hazel.

'Did you or didn't you?'

'Yeah! Did you or didn't you?' repeated Robert Fischer, who had bounced back by now.

'Did I or didn't I *what*?' said Hazel.

'Did you or didn't you say you hate the Yak?' demanded Leon Davis.

'Yeah! Did you or didn't you say—'

Robert Fischer stopped. Hazel had turned one of her fierce gazes on him. He knew what that meant. Leon Davis wasn't always around to protect him.

'What difference does it make to you?' said Hazel, turning back to Leon.

'A lot of difference!'

'Like what?'

'Yeah, like what?' repeated Marcus Bunn, standing just behind Hazel.

'You've never liked the Yak, anyway,' said Hazel.

'Yeah, you've never liked the—'

'Neither have you, Marcus!' said Leon.

Marcus didn't answer that. Suddenly there was silence. Behind Leon Davis stood Robert Fischer, Hamish Rae, Sophie Wigg and Paul Boone. Behind Hazel stood Marcus Bunn, Mandy Furstow, Alli Reddick and Maurice Tobbler, who was known as Cobbler, because it rhymed with his name and because he always took such a long time to consider everything. Others stood close by, not yet having made up their minds which side to join.

'Well?' said Leon. 'Did you say you hate the Yak or didn't you?'

Hazel glanced around. Every face was turned towards her, every eye was watching. Marcus peered at her, waiting to hear the reply.

'Yes,' she said. 'I mean . . . No!'

'*Yes?*'

'*No?*'

There was uproar. Hazel's supporters were shouting at Leon, Leon's supporters were shouting at her. The others were just shouting. A fight would have been certain to follow, even though everyone was already late for school, if Mr Volio, just at that moment, hadn't appeared from the direction of his bakery.

'What's this?' he asked loudly, as he ran towards them. 'What's this? A discussion? Excellent. It's wonderful to see children discussing things. A peaceful discussion. Wonderful!' He walked right up to Hazel and Leon and laid a hand firmly on their shoulders. 'But now that you've had your discussion, it's time to get to school, isn't it?'

'Hazel told the Yak she hates him,' said Leon. He pointed his finger. 'She said she hates all his kind!'

Mr Volio took hold of Leon's pointing hand and lowered it firmly. 'Hazel wouldn't say something like that, would you, Hazel?'

Hazel bit her lip. She was starting to realise something. Her perfect plan to shame Mr Davis hadn't just gone wrong last night. It was *still* going wrong.

She looked up at Mr Volio. The baker was smiling trustfully at her. Hazel tried to smile back.

Hazel Green knew when trouble was brewing. She had so much experience of trouble, she could *feel* when it was starting. And the feeling she had now was quite disturbing. If her experience was anything to judge by, the trouble in this case wasn't over. It was just beginning!

10

That evening, Hazel waited in her room. She didn't know exactly what she was waiting *for*, but she knew something was coming. Somewhere out there, it was making its way towards her.

There are times when you can do just about anything and no one seems to care, and there are times when no one lets you get away with the tiniest thing. When you're as experienced as Hazel, you have a pretty good idea which one it's going to be. This didn't feel like one of those times when nobody cares.

To put it bluntly, Hazel Green wasn't the kind of person whom other people ignore. It wasn't her fault, that's just how she was. Everyone who lived in the Moodey Building knew her, every one of the shopkeepers on the ground floor was accustomed to seeing her around. Everyone had an opinion about her. When she had decided that children should take part in the parade on Frogg Day, for example, there were some who praised her, and some who criticised her, but no one failed to notice what she was doing. They talked about her that time, as well.

If it had been Marcus Bunn who told the Yak he didn't like his kind of people, it's possible that Mrs Burston wouldn't have paid any attention. If she had paid attention, it's possible she wouldn't have bothered rehearsing the story with Manfred, or telling it to her friends. It wouldn't have *been* much of story. But it was a story when it was Hazel Green! And if only half the people in the Moodey Building knew about it when Hazel set off for school in the morning, just about the whole building knew about it by the time she came home that afternoon.

Just about the whole building, but not every last person. Hazel's parents didn't know. She could see that as soon as she came home. But that didn't reassure her. Parents were always the last to know anything, at least Hazel's parents were. Hazel didn't know whether this was because people didn't tell them things, or because they never listened. Yet even they would find out eventually. Well, they mightn't, but that was only a *possibility*, and hardly a *probability*, as the Yak would say, and Hazel didn't count on it.

She didn't feel like going outside. It was better to be here, she thought, when whatever it was that she was waiting for finally arrived. She lay on her bed and stared at the ceiling. The ceiling had a tiny crack running across it, not much bigger than a hair, like a river seen from high in an aeroplane. Hazel knew it well, she knew the angle of every slight turning it took as it made its way from one side of the room to the other. For some reason, she began to think about the Carivari, which was the competition for caricaturists that was held once a year in Victor Square. A big platform was constructed, and on it would sit five famous people in front of the best caricaturists in the city. The caricaturists had to draw each of the five personalities, and then their drawings were judged, and the winner had his name inscribed on a famous silver cup that had been modelled with a crack in the side of it, because it was suppposed to be a caricature of a trophy. But the best part of the Carivari was when the caricaturists were waiting for the judges to decide on the winner. They came down into the crowd with their easels and pencils and did caricatures of people for free. Hazel already had three caricatures from previous years, even though they weren't at all easy to get, because everyone wanted one and you had to be an expert in shoving and pushing and wiggling through the crowd. Poor old Marcus Bunn didn't have even one.

Suddenly Hazel got up and took the caricatures from her cupboard. They were stored inside a cardboard tube and she unrolled them and spread them out on her bed and held down the corners with erasers and pencil cases and other things from her desk. The one from last year showed her holding a lollipop. Her head was big and her whole body was tiny, of course, which is the way caricaturists draw, and she was pinching the stick of the lollipop between thumb and forefinger of her tiny little hand, but the head of the lollipop itself, like her own head, was enormous. It was so big it could have been a mirror. As far as Hazel could remember, she hadn't been holding a lollipop at the time. Where did the caricaturist get the idea? This was her favourite one, anyway, she always thought it was better than the others. Well, almost always. She sighed. Today, it didn't seem so clever. She wasn't in the mood to appreciate it.

The phone rang. Hazel heard her mother answer it

in the corridor outside. Hazel held her breath. Her mother talked, listened, talked again. Then her voice stopped. Hazel waited. Nothing happened. She glanced at the caricatures again. Then she rolled them up and put them away.

What to do? She picked up a book and lay down and began to read it, holding it up above her face in front of the river that ran across the ceiling. But after a minute she stopped and found she couldn't remember a single word she'd read. *This* was interesting. How could you read and not remember anything? It was as if your mind were divided up into two parts, and one of them was reading and the other was thinking about something altogether different. Or maybe it was just your eyes that were reading, and the words didn't even get into your mind. Hazel frowned. She rolled over and propped herself on her elbows and began to read again, very slowly, trying to *feel* when the words got past her eyes. She moved from one word to the next. No. She couldn't tell exactly when it happened. Perhaps it hadn't happened. Perhaps this time she was concentrating *too* hard. When she came to the end of the paragraph, she still couldn't remember what she'd read!

She tossed the book down on her bed. Part of her mind was thinking about something else, that was for sure! She threw herself back and stared up at the ceiling once more. Suddenly it seemed that her room was the only place where she was safe, where no one wanted to accuse her. Even the telephone outside would start to bring accusations, sooner or later.

The waiting was the worst part. Waiting, Hazel had found, was never pleasant, and that was why she always tried to do as little of it as possible.

The river above her snaked across the ceiling. Hazel tried to imagine what it would be like if it were a real river, if you could get closer and closer to it just as if you were coming down through the air, and you'd start to see sunlight glinting and ripples in the water and rocks in the bottom and all of it would be coming fast towards you and then . . . *splash* . . . you'd be in it! But for some reason she suddenly imagined there might be crocodiles in the water, or piranha fish, or some other animal that would eat you alive. It was strange, this was the first time she could remember having thought there might be crocodiles or piranha fish in the river that ran across the top of her room. She began to wonder why she had suddenly—

Hazel stopped wondering. The doorbell had just rung.

It was Hazel's mother who came to get her. Three visitors were waiting in the living room, all sitting on the sofa. There was Mrs Steene, who owned the art supplies shop on the ground floor. She was the shopkeepers' representative on the Moodey Building Committee. In the middle was Mr Lamberto, who lived with his mother and four cats on the eighth floor. And beside him was Mr Davis, who was, of course, the head of the Committee.

Hazel's father was sitting on a chair opposite the sofa. When Hazel came in, everyone looked at her. Hazel's mother put her arm around Hazel's shoulder. There was a heavy silence in the room. Hazel didn't like the feel of it.

Mr Davis glanced at Hazel's father. He cleared his throat meaningfully.

'Hazel,' said Hazel's father, 'we have some visitors who have been telling us something about you that is a little bit . . . well, it's a little bit . . .'

'It's a little bit unpleasant,' boomed Mr Davis, who was only waiting for a chance to start speaking. 'In fact, it's more than a little bit unpleasant. As I said already, normally we wouldn't be coming to talk to you, Mr and Mrs Green. Children will have fights, of course. We all understand that. Even my boys occasionally get into trouble.'

'We wouldn't want to worry you if we didn't think it was *absolutely* necessary,' added Mrs Steene crisply.

'None of us wants to make things any more difficult than they are,' said Mr Lamberto, blinking.

Mr Davis glared at the other two. Mr Lamberto blinked a few more times and was silent.

Mr Davis cleared his throat again. 'The point is, the whole building has heard about this and everybody feels that something must be done. It wasn't just a regular fight. Oh no, Mr and Mrs Green. If only it had been. If *only* it had been. I didn't see it all myself, of course, but Mrs Burston says that some of the things your daughter said, well, they just can't be repeated.'

'Like what?' said Hazel's mother.

'Mrs Burston couldn't bring herself to say.'

'Hazel?' said Hazel's father.

Well, it was about time, thought Hazel, that someone had started to talk to *her!* She was beginning to think she might as well go back to her room.

Unfortunately, there wasn't very much for her to say. She shrugged. How was she supposed to know what Mrs Burston heard? She couldn't remember seeing her there. And even if Mrs Burston had been in the lobby, the fight that Mrs Burston had witnessed, to judge by the rumours Hazel had heard from the other Moodey kids, bore very little resemblance to anything that *she* had been involved in.

'I know this must be very difficult for you, Mr and Mrs Green,' said Mr Davis, 'but everybody feels that something must be done. We can't have the children going around and saying things like that in the lobby for everyone to hear. What will people think of the Moodey Building? Do you realise this is the building where Victor Frogg was born? Victor Frogg, Mr and Mrs Green, the Father of our Nation! We have a reputation to uphold. We have a responsibility. A responsibility that the entire nation, in its hopes, in its dreams, looks to us to . . .'

Mr Davis kept going like that for a while. He was a lawyer, of course, and once he had begun a speech, he inevitably continued until he could have brought it to an end at least three times.

'I'm sure it wasn't as bad as Mrs Burston thought,' said Hazel's mother eventually, when Mr Davis paused for breath. 'She must have misheard. And everyone knows that Mrs Burston does sometimes . . .'

'What?' demanded Mr Davis sharply.

'She does *exaggerate* sometimes.'

'Mrs Green! It's not Mrs Burston who's on trial here. If we are to judge, let us judge the point in question. Whether Mrs Burston exaggerates is not the point in question. The point here is what your daughter said. The point here is that we can't have children saying they don't like other kinds of people in the Moodey Building, the birthplace of Victor Frogg, Mr and Mrs Green, the Father of our Nation. The point here is what you're going to *do* about it!' And Mr Davis thumped his fist on the armrest of the sofa, dramatically, as he might have thumped his fist when making a speech in court.

There was silence. Mrs Steene put her nose in the air. Mr Lamberto blinked. Mr Davis folded his arms and looked around self-righteously. Hazel couldn't believe it! She had listened to his speech about the Moodey Building, she had listened to his speech about who was on trial, and all the time she had been wondering: how could he sit there criticising her for saying exactly the same thing *he* had said to Mr Egozian? How could he deceive people like that? She was getting angrier and angrier. How could Mr Davis dare to demand what her parents were going to do about it? They ought to go and find *his* parents and demand the same thing. If he said anything else, she thought, just the tiniest thing, she wouldn't be able to stop herself. She'd tell everyone *exactly* what happened . . .

'Well?' demanded Mr Davis. 'Would you answer our question, Mr Green? What are you—'

That was it! Hazel couldn't hold back any longer. She turned to her parents. 'All right! Do you want to know why I did it? I don't hate the Yak. He's one of my best friends, and I'm his *only* friend. I still am. You want to know why I did it? It was him!' She threw out her hand and pointed at Mr Davis. 'It was you, Mr Davis. Last week you told Mr Egozian you didn't like him or his kind of people. You didn't think anyone heard, did you, because it was so early in the morning? Well, I heard. I was up. And if it's good enough for you, Mr Davis,' Hazel demanded, 'why shouldn't I say it as well?'

Hazel stopped. There was an icy silence. Not even Mr Lamberto blinked. As the seconds passed, Mr Davis' face went red. It went redder and redder. Suddenly, he shot to his feet.

'Green!' he bellowed at Hazel's father. 'I've never heard such a thing. Are you going to sit there and let your daughter speak to me like this? I expect an apology!'

Hazel's father stood up. Everyone else got to their feet as well.

'Well?' demanded Mr Davis.

'Perhaps we should listen to what she has to say . . .' began Mr Lamberto weakly. 'She means well. She's friends with the boy. Maybe she misheard and—'

'Listen to these . . . these . . . *lies*!' exclaimed Mr Davis. 'Never! Green? What are you going to do? The girl's the biggest troublemaker we've ever had in the Moodey Building! It's no wonder if her own parents can't make her apologise when she tells such lies. Well . . . Well, if *you* can't do anything to control her, then *we'll* have to punish her for you!'

And he turned around and stormed off to the front door.

Mrs Steene shook her head primly and marched after Mr Davis.

'I'm sure we can settle this if we just sit down calmly . . .' began Mr Lamberto.

But it was too late. 'Lamberto!' cried Mr Davis from the front door. 'We aren't staying to be insulted further.'

'Oh dear,' said Mr Lamberto, not knowing what to do, and he stayed for another moment, blinking helplessly at Hazel, before he left as well.

Mr Davis could hardly wait until his two fellow Committee members were out of the apartment, so he could have the pleasure of slamming the door behind him.

'Hazel, you'll have to apologise,' said Hazel's mother.

'To who?'

'Mr Davis.'

'Oh, I thought you meant Mrs Burston. Perhaps I didn't speak loudly enough for her to hear all the things I was supposed to have said.'

Hazel's parents didn't reply to that. That was all right. Hazel wouldn't have replied either.

Hazel's father shook his head. 'I don't understand, Hazel. I thought you *liked* Yakov Plonsk. Why were you fighting with him?'

'I wasn't fighting with him. I told you, I was just repeating what Mr Davis had said. If it's good enough for Mr Davis, why shouldn't—'

'Don't keep saying that, Hazel. Please don't say that again.'

'Why not? It's true, isn't it? Why shouldn't I say something if it's true?'

Hazel's parents didn't reply to that either. This time, it was because there *was* no reply, except for the one that was so obvious it didn't even need to be said.

'Even if Mr Davis did say it,' said Hazel's mother, sighing, 'I don't see why you should want to repeat it.'

'But that was the whole point,' Hazel explained. 'I wanted to show him how awful it was. I wanted him to see. I wanted him to feel ashamed. But you know what he did? He just told us to continue outside!'

Hazel's parents looked at each other. Now they *both* sighed.

'You just can't go around accusing people like Mr Davis,' said Hazel's mother. 'Not like that, Hazel. How do you know you're right? Perhaps you did mishear, like Mr Lamberto said.'

Hazel rolled her eyes.

'It's possible, isn't it?' said Hazel's father. 'I'm sure you meant well, Hazel. It's just . . .'

'What?'

'It's just not the way to do things,' said Hazel's mother. She caressed Hazel's head, gazing at her with a troubled expression. 'You just have to learn, Hazel. You'll have to apologise. It's not the way to talk to a man like Mr Davis.'

Mr Davis? Who cared about Mr Davis? Mr Davis didn't seem to care about anyone else, except Victor Frogg, perhaps, the Father of the Nation, and that was only because Victor Frogg was already dead. All he was really worried about was the Moodey reputation. But the Moodey was just a building. It didn't have feelings, it couldn't be hurt by what people said about it.

Hazel started for the door.

'Hazel, where are you going?'

Hazel turned back for a moment. 'They're so concerned, aren't they? They're so worried I might have hurt the Yak's feelings. Do you really think they care?' She shook her head. 'They think I fought with the Yak? They think I upset him by saying such terrible things? I bet not *one* of them has bothered to visit him.'

11

The Yak's mother was wearing a rose-coloured gown and her fingernails were painted rose as well. Her shoes were the colour of dark honey. Her hair was black. She was holding a pair of spectacles with silver frames.

Hazel looked up at her hesitantly. She didn't know what the Yak's mother had heard about the fight in the lobby. Perhaps someone from the Moodey Building Committee *had* come to see the Yak. The Yak's mother put on her spectacles and peered at Hazel. The spectacles were the kind that have lenses of only half the normal size, cut straight along the top. Normally, Hazel saw those kinds of spectacles only on the noses of old people, who had a habit of staring at you over the top of them, as if they didn't really need the lenses at all. That was what the Yak's mother was doing now. It made her look ten years older. It also made her glance seem particularly penetrating. But when you think you've got some explaining to do, any glance seems penetrating.

'Mrs Plonsk,' Hazel blurted out. 'I don't know what people have been telling you, but—'

'You don't like them?' said the Yak's mother, taking off the spectacles. 'You're right. I've been trying to convince myself, but I don't really like them either.' She examined them for another moment, and then looked back at Hazel. 'Are you here to see Yakov? He's working. Go into the front room and I'll get him.'

So no one had been here! No one from the Committee had bothered to visit the Yak or his mother.

Whatever the Yak had been working on, Hazel could see he was *still* working on it when he sat down in front of her. It was probably a mathematical problem that he was trying to solve. The Yak didn't need pen or paper to work on mathematical problems, like a normal person. He could do everything in his head. Of course, this was quite an extraordinary ability, which very few people possessed, as Hazel knew. But extraordinary abilities weren't necessarily *good*, not all the time, anyway. And the Yak had an extraordinary ability to let his extraordinary abilities get in the way of all kinds of ordinary things, like having a conversation in his front room, for example.

He said hello, but almost as soon as he had said it, he was thinking about the problem again. Hazel could tell.

At first Hazel didn't interrupt him. When the Yak was thinking about something, he concentrated so hard that he lost awareness of anything else. You could stare right at him, and he'd just go on concentrating as if you didn't exist at all. There would be just a hint of a frown on his pointy face, and his eyes would be focussed somewhere in front of him, not far from his toes, to judge from their direction. Recently she had invented a name for him when he was doing this: the Amazingly Motionless Yak. She hadn't told him this name, of course. He breathed, obviously, and occasionally he blinked, so he wasn't Completely Motionless, but he certainly was Amazingly Motionless, compared with the way most people fidgeted and jumped as soon as they realised someone else was looking at them.

The Amazingly Motionless Yak could probably stay Motionless for hours. But Hazel had never tested how long he could go on for—a couple of minutes was more than enough!

Hazel clapped her hands, as she had once seen a hypnotist clap to wake people out of a trance.

The Yak kept staring.

'Yakov! Yakov Plonsk!'

The Yak moved his eyes in her direction. His head didn't turn.

'Wait,' he whispered, and his eyes moved back to focus in front of his toes.

He concentrated for another couple of minutes. Hazel swung her legs impatiently. Finally the frown of concentration on his face relaxed, and he looked around.

'I'm very good to you, you know, Yakov,' said Hazel, as soon as she saw that he was listening. 'Most other people wouldn't let you sit there like that until you'd finished whatever you were thinking about.'

'Most other people wouldn't come to disturb me in the first place,' the Yak pointed out.

True, thought Hazel. But only the Yak would think this was a good thing. Most people would think it was a terrible thing if they had no friends who ever bothered to visit them, even if it meant disturbing them once in a while.

'What were you thinking about?'

The Yak shook his head. 'It's complicated, Hazel.'

Hazel waited.

'I was thinking about the quotients of derivatives of indeterminate polynomials.'

'Oh, those!' said Hazel. 'I used to think about them, but I found it got tedious.'

The Yak stared at her severely.

Hazel yawned. 'Well, you should tell me when you think you've worked something out, and I'll let you know whether I agree.'

The Yak crossed his arms. 'Last time, Hazel, you came to tell me you didn't like me. Now you've come to make fun of me. I get that all day at school. I don't need more of it at home.'

'I didn't come to make fun of you. I'm sorry. It's just . . .'

'What?'

'It's just you're so easy to make fun of!' blurted out Hazel, and she burst into laughter.

The Yak watched her silently.

Hazel stopped laughing. 'All right, Yakov. You're not *so* easy to make fun of. I'm just very good at doing it. It's like you with your mathematical problems. I'm just naturally good at making fun of people.'

The Yak knew that already. After all, who was it who had made up his name, the Yak? Hazel Green! And apparently it didn't occur to her that a person might not want to be known by the name of hairy Tibetan beasts who were probably covered in fleas. But that had happened before Hazel had become friends with him, and the Yak continued to be friends with her only because he doubted she'd make up a name like that for him now. No, that was one thing he was pretty sure of, she had stopped making up silly names for him.

'It's true, Yakov. It's this natural ability I have, I'm good at making fun of people. Sometimes,' she whispered, 'I think it's a curse.' Hazel's eyes went wide, and she kept looking at him with such a terrified, spooky expression on her face that in the end he couldn't keep himself from grinning.

His pointy face scrunched up, and he shook his head, and after a moment both he and Hazel were laughing.

'Listen, Yakov,' said Hazel eventually, 'I did come for a serious reason. I wanted to see if you were all right.'

The Yak shrugged. 'Why shouldn't I be all right?'

'Well, everyone's saying I had a real fight with you, and that I really hate you and your kind of people.'

'Really? Is that what they're saying?'

Hazel shook her head in disbelief. Didn't the Yak know anything about what was going on?

'They're exaggerating everything, Yakov. They're making it sound awful.'

'But it did sound awful. That was the whole idea, remember?'

'No, they're making it sound really, really awful. I just wanted to make sure . . . I don't want you to feel bad, that's all, *whatever* you hear people say.'

'I won't feel bad,' said the Yak. 'I know what the real reason was. We were trying to make Mr Davis feel ashamed. It was quite a good plan, actually, despite the fifteen things that could go wrong with it. It didn't quite work, but it's not a tragedy. At least you tried, Hazel Green.'

Hazel smiled. '*We* tried, Yakov. It wasn't just me.'

'That's right. And I'm glad we tried. But it didn't work. That's it.'

No, that wasn't *quite* it.

'I told them what happened,' said Hazel. 'I told them why we did it.'

'Good,' said the Yak. 'Now everyone knows. Maybe Mr Davis will feel ashamed after all.'

'They don't believe me, Yakov. I told them everything. I told them what I heard Mr Davis say. And even if they do believe me, they think I shouldn't have said anything about it.'

'But that isn't logical. You told the truth.'

Hazel shrugged.

The Yak frowned. The frown on his face got deeper and deeper. Soon he looked as if he was in real pain. Hazel watched him. Something was causing havoc in that mathematical brain of his. Order was being disturbed!

'Why shouldn't you say something if it's the truth?' he asked, still struggling to understand. 'The truth is always right. It's the *truth*. The truth should always be told. From that premise, it follows that to hide the truth is always wrong.'

'I *told* them. I told Mr Davis to his face!' cried Hazel, and she almost jumped up off the sofa when she remembered how she'd done it.

'And that didn't help?' inquired the Yak disbelievingly.

'It made it worse!'

'Very strange,' murmured the Yak. 'Very, very strange . . .'

The Yak shook his head with an expression of dismay and confusion. Suddenly Hazel liked him more than she had ever liked him before. He really did think it was strange. He really couldn't understand why an adult would be angry with a child who said something against him, even if it was the truth. Anyone else would have understood. She understood, even though she *was* that child—it was the injustice of it that made her so angry. But perhaps the world of mathematics wasn't like that. Perhaps, in the world of mathematics, adults didn't get angry with children who contradicted them. But real life wasn't like mathematics, and mathematics certainly wasn't like real life, as she had told the Yak many times before.

Hazel gazed at the Yak. Suddenly he seemed like a very small, defenceless person who lived in his own little world, and she wanted to protect him.

'Perhaps you should tell them again,' said the Yak.

Hazel shook her head. She didn't think *that* would be a particularly good idea. When people were angry with you for what you had said, they were rarely happier when you repeated it.

'Then what are you going to do?'

'They want me to apologise,' said Hazel.

'Apologise? But you'd be apologising for telling the truth!' The Yak jumped out of his chair and started walking agitatedly amongst the sofas. 'Apologise? For telling the truth? *Apologise?*' He stopped and turned to

Hazel. 'Hazel, you can't apologise for that! It's a matter of principle! If you start apologising for telling the truth, where will it stop? Before long we'll be apologising whenever an equation turns out to have no solution! We'll be apologising whenever a fraction gives a recurring decimal!'

Hazel stared at the Yak. She shook her head. What world *did* he live in?

'We'll be apologising whenever a derivative can't—'

'Yakov, I'm not going to apologise! Of course I'm not.' It was a matter of principle, the Yak was right. Besides, the idea of saying sorry to Mr Davis, after all the false, deceitful things he had just said in her very own apartment, in front of her very own parents, made her sick. 'I'm not going to apologise, but they'll punish me, Yakov. Mr Davis said they would.'

'What are they going to do?' asked the Yak quietly, and he came back to sit in front of Hazel.

Hazel shrugged. 'They're probably deciding right now.'

'But Hazel, you're not going to apologise, are you? Truth is the basis of order, and order is the basis of life. Order is eternal, order is—'

'Universal. Yes, I know all that, Yakov. But punishments aren't pleasant.'

The Yak nodded.

Hazel raised an eyebrow. This was interesting! When would a boy like the Yak ever have been punished?

'I mean, I'm assuming they are,' said the Yak. 'I've never actually *been* punished. But logically, they should be. Otherwise, what's the point?'

What a disappointment! It would have just about been worth all this trouble to find out something mischievous the Yak had done in his time. If anyone had asked Hazel about all the occasions she'd been punished, the list would have gone on for hours.

'So, what are you going to do?' said the Yak.

'I don't know,' said Hazel. She thought about it for a moment. 'But if I need help, I know I can rely on you.'

'Hazel . . .'

'Truth, Yakov! Truth. Are you saying you wouldn't help me? You said it yourself, it's a matter of principle. Are you saying you wouldn't bother to defend Truth . . . Order . . . Justice . . . Mathematics . . .' Hazel ran out of words, and desperately tried to think of more.

But she didn't have to bother.

The Yak was on his feet again, and in a flash, he had his finger on his nose, ready to swear.

12

Over the next few days, Hazel discovered something very strange. Her so-called fight with the Yak wasn't just something that happened between two people in a lobby, which another couple of people had seen. No. That may have been how it started, but that wasn't what it became. One of the people who had seen the fight took it out of the lobby with her, and sent it out into the world, and once it got out there, it had a life of its own. It was changed, transformed by others into something people could use, like a tool, or an instrument. And as far as Hazel could tell, they didn't really care about the instrument itself— they only cared about what they could use it *for*.

But even that wasn't the strangest thing about the fight. The strangest thing was that so many people seemed to be *glad* it had happened, so that they could have this instrument in their hands.

They weren't glad about it in an open, honest way. In fact, a big part of this gladness involved pretending that the fight with the Yak was truly awful, perhaps the most awful thing they had ever heard of in their lives. But you could see, even as they spoke, how much they actually enjoyed talking about it, and there wasn't a hint of regret in the tone of their voice or the look in their eye. Pretending it was awful was just their way of using it as an instrument against Hazel. Because it really was awful. Awful, awful, *awful*. The fact that Hazel had insulted

Mr Davis afterwards simply made it more *awful*. Needless to say, they enjoyed talking about how awful that was as well.

Leon Davis and his supporters were the biggest culprits. The walk to and from school each day was one long procession of taunts and provocation. She only had to glance at someone for Robert Fischer to shout: 'Watch out! Hazel doesn't like your kind. She's giving you the evil eye!' Robert Fischer didn't even know what the evil eye was. Or she only had to start talking to someone and Leon Davis would shout: 'Watch out! You never know what she'll say next. She'd insult you to your face if she thought it would save her skin!' Which is exactly what Leon himself would do.

But Hazel didn't tell Leon that he could start with *himself* if he was looking for liars, and she didn't tell Robert that the only evil eyes she could see were the ones in his own head—which is what she normally would have done. She didn't think it was necessarily a good idea to start any more fights just at the moment, and besides, she wasn't sure what her own supporters would do if she did.

That was another strange thing. In a way, her own friends were glad about her fight with the Yak as well. No one could understand why she ever liked him in the first place. Marcus Bunn was gladdest of all. To tell the truth, he was quite jealous of the Yak, because Hazel had been so friendly with him. As far as he was concerned, Hazel's fight with the Yak was the best thing that could have happened.

But even Marcus wasn't happy with what Hazel was rumoured to have said. The Yak . . . what kind of a target was he? He wasn't like Leon Davis. You could hardly expect the Yak to defend himself from someone like Hazel. If she wanted to stop being friends with him, she could have just stopped being friends. She didn't need to shout all those awful things at him. Besides, it was one thing to call someone a liar, or a cheater. But to say you didn't like their *kind*? That wasn't the same. Somehow, it seemed much nastier. No one could help being born as what they were.

So even though Marcus didn't like the Yak, he didn't want to believe that Hazel had said those things. Neither did Cobbler, Mandy Furstow, Alli Reddick or any of the others who were usually on her side. Hazel wouldn't want to have believed that one of her friends would say something like that either. That was the whole point! Yet the others didn't seem to understand. When she explained that she was only repeating what Mr Davis had said himself, they groaned. 'Don't blame Mr Davis,' Mandy Furstow advised her, 'it's always better to own up in the end.' Cobbler would scratch his head, frowning, and say: 'You still haven't apologised, Hazel? Is that true? You *still* haven't apologised?'

And it wasn't only the Moodey children who seized hold of the fight and used it like a weapon. For a lot of the adults, too, Hazel's deed seemed to have turned into an instrument, which they wielded with the same tone of pretended outrage and the same glint of hidden enjoyment that came from Leon Davis and his gang.

Mr Winkel, for example, who disliked all children, and Hazel most of all, because she had outsmarted him when the Moodey children wanted to march in the Frogg Day parade, came out of his leather goods store especially to find her. Normally, Mr Winkel didn't let even let children into his shop, much less go out to find them. But there he was one afternoon, marching after her up the pavement, as if he had been standing and peering out of his window just to see when she walked by. With his bald head, and his big, bony nose, and his bushy eyebrows and his eyes narrowed in pursuit, he swept towards her like an eagle swooping on its prey.

'Hazel Green!' he exclaimed when he reached her. 'Stop there. Stop right there. I've something to say to you.'

Hazel stopped.

'I just wanted to tell you that what you said to the poor boy . . . that boy . . . what's his name?'

'Yakov?'

'That's right. What you said to that poor boy, Yakov, was the nastiest, most horrible thing I've ever heard. I always knew what you were really like, Hazel Green. Now *everyone* knows.' And Mr Winkel folded his arms, and his bushy eyebrows went right up on his forehead, as if to say, 'So there!'

Hazel looked at him. 'No,' she said after a moment, 'only you know.'

Mr Winkel's eyebrows plunged in a frown. 'What does that mean?' he demanded.

Hazel shrugged. She started walking again.

'Hazel Green! Come back here and explain!'

But Hazel didn't go back to explain. For a start, she would have had to think of an explanation, and for a finish, Mr Winkel probably wouldn't have understood it anyway. She didn't care about Mr Winkel, or about Mr Murray, the rival baker to Mr Volio, who cornered her a couple of days after Mr Winkel's ambush and just *had* to tell her what he thought, or about any of the other adults who wanted to use the fight like an instrument to make her feel bad. She didn't care about people who were secretly glad at something as awful as what she was supposed to have done. If people don't like you already, what difference does it make if they dislike you a bit more?

No, the ones Hazel cared about were the ones who weren't glad at all, either secretly or otherwise. They were the ones, she knew, who were really hurt to think she could have done what everyone was saying. Like Mr Petrusca, the fishmonger, who looked at her with an expression full of pain and incomprehension when she went into his shop to say hello one day. He glanced up and saw her while he was filleting a fish, and almost cut his thumb off with his razor-sharp knife. And then, of course, there was Mr Volio . . .

Mr Volio shook his head. He looked down at his kneading table, where there was a big lump of dough, and shook his head again.

'I believed you, Hazel,' he murmured, 'that's the thing.'

'I know,' said Hazel. She felt so bad she could barely speak.

It was late in the afternoon. Soon Mr Volio would start the furnace, and the great brick walls of his baking oven would begin to gather heat, and after that the apprentices and the other bakers would arrive and there would be clatter and commotion as the night's work commenced. But for now the bakery was quiet, and there was no one there but Hazel and Mr Volio.

Mr Volio began to slap the dough on the kneading table. Expertly, he slapped and slapped, then raised the dough, turned it, twirled it, threw it down and started slapping again.

'Do you remember that time I thought you stole the recipe for the Chocolate Dipper?' he said, watching his hands as they worked the dough. 'You told me you didn't steal it, and I didn't believe you. I didn't *want* to believe you, because the truth was worse. Deep down, I knew you weren't lying, but it was too painful to admit to myself what had really happened, that one of my own apprentices had betrayed me.' Mr Volio worked and worked at the dough, the balls of his hands pounding against the table. 'I've never forgotten that, Hazel. It taught me a lesson. So when I found you the other morning, when you and Leon were about to start fighting, I believed you. I told Leon off. But Leon was right. *You* were the one I should have told off. You said you hadn't said those things to Yakov, but you had.' He looked up. 'I trusted you . . . and you lied. This time, *you* betrayed me.'

'No, Mr Volio.'

'No?' Mr Volio shook his head. 'Yes, I think.' He pounded his fists into the dough, knuckles first.

'Mr Volio, I did say those things, but I didn't mean them.'

'Who can tell what anyone *means*, Hazel? It's the things we say that count.'

'But Yakov knew I didn't mean them. We planned it. He knew everything I was going to say before I said it.'

'More lies, Hazel?' said Mr Volio wearily.

'No!' Hazel cried. 'It's true. It's *true*, Mr Volio. Ask him yourself if you don't believe me. Look, I'll take you if you want. I'll take you up to him right now.'

The baker stopped kneading. He gazed doubtfully at Hazel Green.

'If you're lying to me again, Hazel . . .'

'I'm not lying. I'd never lie to you, Mr Volio.'

Mr Volio ran his fingers through his thick black moustache.

'All right,' he said eventually. 'So the Yak knew. Do you think I understand any of this?'

Hazel shook her head. 'I'm not saying it's easy to understand, Mr Volio.'

'Why doesn't this surprise me, Hazel?'

'It's all because I heard Mr Davis say—'

'Yes. We've heard about that as well, Hazel. Accusing him in public, a man like Mr Davis.'

'But it's true! It's all true.'

'So what?' cried Mr Volio. 'Who cares if it's true? Do you have proof? Hazel, do you think you can accuse a person in public without proof? A person like Mr Davis, no less. What would the world be like if everyone went around doing that?'

'Lots of people do it,' said Hazel.

'See!' exclaimed Mr Volio, and he pounded the dough again.

The baker put his hands on his hips. He was breathing heavily. His moustache was full of pale crumbs that he had left behind when he ran his fingers through the bristles. Finally he picked up the dough with one hand. It hung limply from his fingers.

'Look what you've made me do. Dough should be kneaded firmly but steadily, and not too much. Look at this. Look! What can I do with it?'

'Throw it out?'

'Throw it out, she says,' muttered Mr Volio, and he walked over to a big bin beside the refrigerator and did exactly that.

'When my father gets angry he likes to go for a swim,' said Hazel.

'He swims, I knead,' replied Mr Volio. 'I'm a baker, not a fish.'

He sat down beside the kneading table.

'Oh, Hazel. What are we going to do with you?'

13

'Mr Volio's right,' said Mrs Gluck. 'And your parents are right as well, Hazel. You can't go around saying things like that about a man like Mr Davis.'

'Mr Davis! Mr Davis!' muttered Hazel. 'No one believes me because it's Mr Davis. I bet if it was anyone else, no one would care. What's so special about Mr *Davis?*'

'Nothing,' said Mrs Gluck. 'You're right. You can't go around saying things like that about anyone. You can't just go accusing people without proof, Hazel, no matter who they are. You ought to know that already.'

'I bet if I said it was Mr *Egozian*, no one would get upset,' muttered Hazel. 'I don't think anyone would care at all.'

Hazel picked up a tulip that was lying on Mrs Gluck's worktable. She did know about proof. Of course she knew. She had never planned to accuse Mr Davis, with proof or without it. He was supposed to feel so ashamed that he would accuse himself . . . or at least apologise to Mr Egozian . . . or something like that. It was only when he hadn't, and people demanded to know why she had fought with the Yak, that she had found herself accusing him. And whose fault was that? Anyone but Mr Davis would have had the decency to feel ashamed, Hazel was certain. No one else would have just told her to keep on shouting at the Yak *outside*.

'I used to have a customer who was a lawyer,' Mrs Gluck said. 'Have I ever told you about him, Hazel? Mr O'Riordan, his name was. Proof was everything to Mr O'Riordan. *Don't worry about a motive,* he used to say, *get proof!*' Mrs Gluck said it in a deep voice, just as a lawyer might, with a great deal of emphasis, and then she chuckled. 'He used to tell me about his cases sometimes. Not everything, of course, that wouldn't have been right. And he always ended by saying, *Don't worry about a motive. Get proof!* He'd come in now and again to buy a bunch of roses for his wife. Not regularly, just when he felt like it. Always something simple, nothing fancy. Just a bunch of roses, sometimes yellow, sometimes white.'

'I wasn't worrying about a motive,' muttered Hazel.

'I know. I know you weren't,' said Mrs Gluck. 'When we were talking about proof, it just reminded me of him, that's all.'

Hazel sighed. She turned the tulip over in her hands. It was a young tulip, and its orange petals were still tightly gathered. The funny thing about tulips, she thought, was that they looked best when they were hardly open, but once their petals had started to spread, they soon looked ragged. Take lilies, on the other hand. Lily buds were unimpressive, and only after they had fully opened did they blaze with colour. Tulips, Hazel decided, were the exception. Most flowers looked their best after they'd opened completely. And Hazel looked around the room, at all the vases and buckets of flowers, tulips and lilies and gerberas and zinnias and roses and . . . Roses? There was a vase of lovely delicate rosebuds, yellow, orange and white, right next to a bucket brimming with bright, luscious, open red roses. Now, which of *those* was more attractive? That was a good question . . .

'Hazel?'

Hazel looked back. Mrs Gluck was ready for the tulip that Hazel was holding. The arrangement she was making included white ranunculi and yellow freesias, and she was completing it with the orange tulips. She had already slotted two tulips into place. Hazel handed the flower over, and now Mrs Gluck positioned it in the bunch, and deftly bound the stems with twine.

'Would you mind, Hazel?' she said, and held the arrangement out towards her.

Hazel took the bouquet and went to place it in a vase on one of the shelves against the wall. Mrs Gluck consulted her order book. Then she got up and began to walk around the room, collecting flowers for the next arrangement. Soon she was back at the table and had started work again.

'Mrs Gluck?' said Hazel.

'Yes.'

'Why weren't you angry with me?'

Mrs Gluck looked up.

'When you heard what I said to the Yak, I mean. Why weren't you angry?'

Mrs Gluck laughed, and continued working. 'I heard it from Mrs Burston. She came into the shop and told me herself. She made Sophie call me in from the back just so she could tell me.'

'But Mrs Burston was there. She heard what I said!'

'But we all know Mrs Burston, don't we?' said Mrs Gluck. 'From what I understand, she heard quite a few things you *didn't* say as well.'

'No, really, Mrs Gluck. What if it hadn't been Mrs Burston? What if it had been . . . say . . . Mr Petrusca?'

'Still wouldn't have believed it,' said Mrs Gluck briskly.

'But Mr Petrusca doesn't exaggerate.'

'But he can make a mistake. I would have said to myself, it must be a mistake.'

'But it wasn't a mistake. I did say those things.'

'You said them, but you didn't say them for the reasons Mrs Burston assumed. You didn't mean what she thought you meant. So it was a misunderstanding. And a misunderstanding's as good as a mistake—sometimes better.'

Hazel grinned. Mrs Gluck held up a lily and examined it critically.

'What do you think, Hazel? I want a light cream. Very light. Just the faintest off from white. I'm not sure if this is the right one, after all.'

'Shall I try to find you another one?'

Mrs Gluck nodded. Hazel went to the bucket of lilies. She picked two others out and showed them to Mrs Gluck. The florist hesitated for a moment.

'That one,' she said.

Hazel put the others back. 'I still don't see how you could have been so sure,' she said, when she returned to the table.

'I know exactly the colour I want, Hazel. I can see it in my mind.'

'No, Mrs Gluck! I mean about me. I don't see how you could have been so sure it was a mistake or a misunderstanding. What if it wasn't?'

'But it was.'

'But what it if wasn't?'

'But it *was*, Hazel.' Mrs Gluck shook her head. 'I know you, Hazel Green. I've known you since you were only a tiny little Green thing. I know you're not perfect. I know you get up to mischief. But I know the kind of mischief you would get up to, and the kind you wouldn't. And that's why I'm telling you—I knew.'

Hazel frowned. 'People can change, Mrs Gluck.'

'People *can* change,' said the florist.

'So?' said Hazel.

'So what?'

'How did you know I didn't change?'

Mrs Gluck smiled. She shook her head once more.

Sophie, the girl who served in the front of the shop, appeared in the doorway.

'Mrs Gluck!' she said breathlessly, as if something truly terrible had happened. 'We've run out of gerberas, and I've got a customer who wants half a dozen.'

'There's more here, Sophie.'

'And jonquils, Mrs Gluck, we've almost run out of them. And of course someone just bought all our pink roses.'

Of *course*, thought Hazel.

Mrs Gluck turned to her. 'Hazel, would you mind giving Sophie a hand?'

Hazel got up. It was a strange kind of hand that

Sophie seemed to want, the kind where she got to stand by and watch while Hazel collected all the different flowers she needed. Then it was the kind of hand where Sophie marched back out to the front and Hazel followed with the flowers in her arms.

'I heard they're thinking of a punishment for you, Hazel Green,' whispered Sophie, as soon as they were out of the workroom. 'I heard they're thinking of something *awful.*'

'At least they can think!' Hazel whispered back.

Sophie didn't have time to think of a reply before they were at the wrapping desk in the front of the shop. 'Put them all there,' she said briskly. 'I'll arrange them in a minute.'

This was something that Sophie would never have let Hazel do. Arranging the flowers in the front of the shop, if you believed Sophie, was a job of incredible skill and almost unbelievable complexity, and she spent almost all her time doing it. Not only arranging the flowers, but rearranging them as well, and then disarranging them, so she could rearrange them all over again. In fact, Sophie might easily have spent the whole day hovering over vases and fiddling with bouquets, if not for the customers who kept coming in to disturb her. Like the customer, for example, who wanted the gerberas that Hazel had brought from the back. She was standing right in front of the wrapping desk, waiting to be served.

'You can go now, Hazel,' muttered Sophie out of the corner of her mouth, as she began to wrap the flowers.

Hazel watched her. Sophie was wrapping the gerberas a bit roughly, if you wanted her opinion.

'Hazel!' Sophie glanced at her irritably.

Hazel smiled at the customer. 'I'm waiting,' she explained.

'For what?' said the customer.

'For the day to arrive. It's the day Sophie's waiting for. We're both waiting, in fact.'

'Really?' said the customer, looking interested. 'Is it today?'

'No,' said Hazel, 'it's not today. It's not today, is it, Sophie?'

'I don't know what day you're talking about, Hazel Green. I really don't.'

'The day when the flowers walk out from the back by themselves.'

Sophie glared at Hazel. The customer laughed.

'It's coming, Sophie. Don't worry, that day's coming,' sang Hazel in a high, eerie voice, as she went back to Mrs Gluck's workroom.

'I hope they really punish you, Hazel Green. I hope they think of something really *awful!*' cried Sophie after her.

Mrs Gluck shook her head when Hazel appeared. 'What was that about, Hazel? What did you say to Sophie out there?'

'Nothing, Mrs Gluck.'

'Nothing?'

'Well, not a lot.'

Mrs Gluck chuckled. 'You see, I know you, Hazel Green. I know what you get up to.'

'You don't seem to know Sophie.'

'I do. That's the point.'

Hazel frowned at that, and she looked at Mrs Gluck, wondering what she meant. Then she said: 'Mrs Gluck, you haven't heard what punishment they're planning for me, have you?'

Mrs Gluck shook her head.

'I just wish they'd make up their minds. Do you think it's going to be awful?'

'I hope not.' The florist gazed at Hazel. Suddenly she sat back and folded her arms. 'I can see you're not going to apologise, are you, Hazel?'

Hazel shook her head. 'I can't, Mrs Gluck. It was the truth. It's a matter of principle. The truth is the truth. How can you deny it?'

Mrs Gluck nodded. 'It is a matter of principle. Well, if you're not going to apologise, you have no alternative. You'll need proof, Hazel Green.'

14

Proof.

Easy to say, just one little word. Say it again. Proof. And again. Proof. A silly word. Just a roof with a big P-thing standing in front of it. Silly, very silly. So silly, it was hard to see why anyone would ever need it.

What was *proof*, anyway? Ask the Yak, and he'd tell you it was something on paper, numbers and symbols and formulae, which were all supposed to mean something. To *prove* something. The Yak loved those kinds of proofs, especially proof by subtraction, which was the most elegant kind. That's if you believed the Yak, or even understood what he was talking about. Hazel didn't. Not really. She never understood the lines and lines of numbers and symbols that he was always scribbling. And what use was a proof no one else could understand?

None. Not this time, anyway. It wasn't a Yak-proof she needed, no matter how elegant. She needed something everyone would accept. In short, she needed . . . witnesses!

But that was the really silly thing. *She* was a witness! What more did they want? Yet no one believed her. They believed Mrs Burston, just because she was an old lady who owned a parrot, but they didn't believe her, just because she was a young lady who didn't. She felt like getting that old parrot out of Mrs Burston's apartment and plucking each of its feathers off, one by one, right in front of Mrs Burston's face. That would teach her a lesson. Old Manfred would squawk with pain until he was red in the beak! It wouldn't be very fair on him, though. After all, a parrot can't choose who buys it, and even if it repeats all the rubbish its owner teaches it, you can't really blame it for that. If a human hasn't got enough common sense to think about what it's saying, what can you expect from a bird?

Anyway, plucking Manfred wouldn't really help things. No one believed what Hazel said, and she was the only witness she had. What do you do if no one believes your witness? How do you prove things then?

Another witness!

Another witness. It was obvious. But Hazel didn't *have* another witness. Then again, just because she didn't have another witness *now*, it didn't mean she couldn't get one . . .

The Yak? He was as good as a witness. Hazel had told him exactly what happened, so what was the difference? How would it hurt him to say that he had heard—just passing by, coincidentally, at the time, or putting his head out the window—the things Mr Davis said to Mr Egozian? How *would* it hurt, really? Mr Davis did say those things, after all. And people would believe the Yak, Hazel was sure they would. He was that kind of boy. He was quiet, never got into fights, and apparently had never even been punished. No one would ever suspect he'd make anything up. If she could only convince the Yak to say he'd heard Mr Davis, her problems would be over. It would certainly be a lot more helpful than plucking Mrs Burston's parrot!

The problem was, the Yak would never do it. Hazel knew what he'd do: scrunch up his pointy face and laugh. And when he finished laughing, he'd give her a lecture on Proof, with about fifteen principles and practices. And then he'd start on Witnesses, Honesty and Justice. Why? Because Proof, Witnesses, Honesty and Justice were all parts of Order in the world. Hazel could hear him already. And all she needed, right now, was another lecture on Order from the Order King of Yakland!

Besides, that wasn't really the problem, and Hazel knew it. The reason she refused to apologise to Mr Davis was because all she had done was to tell the truth. So how could she ask the Yak to *lie*?

But it wouldn't be lying, Hazel tried to tell herself. The Yak would be telling what really happened. Mr Davis really did say those things to Mr Egozian.

But the Yak didn't hear them, she replied to herself. *That* would be the lie.

So what? What's one small lie if it helps you get to the truth? Look at the lie Mr Davis is telling, she reminded herself. It's a whopper. He says he didn't say those things at all!

Hazel shook her head. She hated these arguments when Hazel 1 argued with Hazel 2. One of the Hazels always ended up being right, which meant that one of them always ended up being wrong. And the one who was wrong always seemed to be the one she wished was right . . .

Well, she could argue with herself until she was red in the beak, but the fact was plain. If you insisted on your right to tell the truth, you couldn't start using lies to prove your case. It was a matter of principle. And Hazel didn't need the Yak, or Mrs Gluck, or anyone else to tell her that!

But that left her where she had started from. She still needed another witness. Someone who had been there, seen Mr Davis, heard what he had said. But who? Who else might have been up so early in the morning? Mr Volio was up, of course, but he had been outside on the pavement, waiting for her, and wouldn't have heard anything. If he had heard Mr Davis, he'd already have said so. And the other bakers were up, but they were in the bakery. No, there was no one else. Just Mr Davis and Mr Egozian out there in the courtyard, in the early chill of the morning, with no one else around . . .

Mr Egozian. Of course. Mr Egozian himself had been there!

What better witness could you ask for than the very person who was the victim of the crime?

Mr Egozian came out with his broom.

He set to work, as always, at the edge of the courtyard, and progressed methodically, crossing the courtyard from one side to the other, stopping, stooping, gathering the dust, straightening up and starting off again in the opposite direction. Side to side. Side to side. Side to side. It was very calm, very repetitive, very *orderly*.

It made Hazel think of the Yak. Perhaps she should bring the Yak down to watch one day. He might enjoy it. Perhaps she should even introduce him to Mr Egozian.

Gradually the caretaker came closer, sweeping. As he moved along behind the broom, he didn't take his eyes off the ground in front of him.

He arrived beside Hazel. He swept up the dust and emptied it into his bag. But he didn't turn again straight away. He rested his hands on the end of the broom, and his chin on his hands.

Hazel watched him with curiosity.

'Hazel Green, I heard you got into trouble,' he said in his quiet voice.

Hazel grinned. She nodded. 'I'm always getting into trouble, Mr Egozian. It's nothing to worry about.'

'I heard it was because of me.'

'No, Mr Egozian. I just said the wrong thing at the wrong time, that's all.'

'But you said it because of me.'

Hazel shrugged. Who knew why people said things? It was hard enough to work out what people meant by what they said, most of the time, without worrying about why they'd decided to say it.

'I'm sorry about that, Hazel.'

'Well, it's my own fault, Mr Egozian. All I have to do is apologise to Mr Davis and everything will be forgiven. No one seems to care whether I apologise to the Yak, by the way, although I'm supposed to have said the most awful things to him. All they can think about is how I insulted poor Mr Davis.'

'But you're not going to apologise, I heard.'

'No, because I only told the truth.'

Mr Egozian nodded. He looked down thoughtfully at the head of his broom. 'I hear they're going to punish you.'

'Mr Egozian, that's because they don't believe me. If they believed me, they wouldn't want to punish me. That's why I wanted to talk to you again.'

'Oh, so you didn't come here just to watch me sweep?' said the caretaker, smiling.

Hazel grinned. 'No, but I was thinking maybe there's someone who'd like to. He's a friend of mine, a mathematician. Do you know much about mathematics, Mr Egozian?'

Mr Egozian shook his head.

'Doesn't matter,' said Hazel, 'neither do I. Would you mind if I brought him to watch you one day? You see, I think this is exactly the kind of job he'd like, if he wasn't a mathematician. Walking up and down, sweeping carefully. It's a job with a lot of order.'

'I suppose it is,' said Mr Egozian.

'And he likes order, this friend of mine. He's called the Yak, by the way, but you'd better call him Yakov if you meet him. If you could sell order, the Yak would buy it all. He loves it, really.'

Mr Egozian was looking at Hazel quizzically, and for a moment she even suspected that he didn't understand what she meant.

'The problem is, he doesn't often come out of his

apartment.' Hazel got to her feet and pointed. 'Look, that's his window up there, on the third floor. He might even be watching us, although you can't tell, because you can't actually see through it. It's the Laws of Nature that do that, you know. He's going to explain it to me one day, only he doesn't know it yet.'

Mr Egozian glanced at Hazel for a moment. Then he looked back up at the window.

'Mr Egozian,' said Hazel, 'what I really wanted to ask you is . . .'

The caretaker turned to her.

She hesitated. 'It's . . . Won't you tell them what happened?'

Mr Egozian shook his head. 'Don't ask me to do that, Hazel. Please don't ask me.'

'But if only you said what happened, there'd be two of us, and there's only *one* Mr Davis. They'd have to believe us.'

'Would they? Why do they *have* to do anything? Mr Davis could say anything he liked. He could say you misheard. He could say I was lying.'

'But I didn't mishear, did I?'

'But he could *say* it. What would you do then, Hazel? How could you deny it?' Mr Egozian paused. 'Don't you understand? Mr Davis is a respectable man.'

'So are you!'

'I'm a caretaker, Hazel. An old caretaker who comes from another country. Mr Davis is . . . he's a respectable man. He's a lawyer. He makes speeches. People believe him.'

'A respectable man,' muttered Hazel. 'He's a liar. And he's a . . . hater, that's what he is. He hates people for no reason.'

'That's true. He hates my people. I don't know why.' Mr Egozian paused. 'I'll tell you something, Hazel. There was a time—it's not so long ago, in fact, when you think about it—when my people were slaughtered like sheep. A lot of people don't know this, even today. Maybe the people who write the history books don't mention it. Or maybe the world just wants to forget. At the time, there was a war going on. During this war, soldiers would come to the villages and kill every one of my people that they found. Why, Hazel?' Mr Egozian peered at her, as if he couldn't understand. 'Why would people kill like that, even soldiers? Kill women, children? Even today some people deny it happened, or they say it was only a few, or it was only an accident. It wasn't an accident. Two of my grandparents were murdered like that, and four of their children, who would have been my uncles and aunts. Is that an accident?'

Hazel stared at Mr Egozian. 'Where did this happen?' she whispered. 'Not here?'

'No, Hazel. Far away.'

'When was it, Mr Egozian? Was I born?'

The caretaker shook his head. '*I* wasn't born, Hazel. This was almost a century ago now. Still, it's not so long, is it? There are probably still people alive who remember it. My uncles and aunts, the ones who were murdered, they were only small children at the time. I never knew them, only from stories that I heard about them later.'

Hazel was still staring, trying to imagine what Mr Egozian had told her.

'Listen, Hazel,' he said, smiling. 'I'm not telling you this to make you sad. I don't want you to be sad. There are a lot of good things in life that should make you happy. I don't spend all my time thinking about this. But sometimes I do think about it. Someone has to remember what happened. It just shows, people can hate. Some people seem to hate others who aren't like them. Who can understand it? Maybe it's what they're taught. Maybe it's what someone else does to them. Sometimes I think there's a part in each of us that can hate other people. There's a part that can love, and there's also a part that can hate. And if you're taught the wrong thing, or you come across the wrong person, it's the hating part that wins.'

'But you don't hate anyone, do you?' asked Hazel.

'Perhaps I just never came across the wrong person,' replied Mr Egozian.

Hazel gazed at the caretaker. After a moment she shook her head. No! She couldn't imagine Mr Egozian ever telling anyone that he hated them, the way Mr Davis had. Perhaps Mr Davis hadn't meant it, either. But then why had he denied saying it? If it was some kind of joke, he should have admitted it. And if it was a joke, he certainly hadn't explained it to Mr Egozian!

'Being told that someone doesn't like me or my

people,' said Mr Egozian, 'I can live with that. I've been through worse, believe me. I'm sixty-two years old. I'm not a boy. When someone says that to me, I look at him and I think: do you think you're hurting me? *You're* the one who's being hurt. You don't hate me, you hate *yourself*.'

'Is that what you've always done?' said Hazel.

'As I said, I'm not a boy any more.'

'But you fought back, didn't you? When you were a boy you fought back.'

Mr Egozian shook his head. 'Not really. Some of my friends did, sometimes, but they always ended up getting hurt. Most of us didn't. Sometimes I wanted to fight back, I wished I was brave enough. Now, I don't even wish that any more. I was sensible. I can see I wouldn't have changed anything.'

'Really, Mr Egozian?'

Mr Egozian didn't reply. He looked down at his broom for a moment. Then he turned to Hazel once more. 'I'm sorry, Hazel. I can't help you. If I say anything about Mr Davis, that'll be the end of me. He'll get rid of me for sure. And what other job will I get? I'll have to go and live with my daughter and her family.'

'But he'll get rid of you anyway, if he hates you so much,' said Hazel.

'Let him find the way, then. I'm not going to open the door for him!' Mr Egozian smiled. 'Hazel, you should apologise if you want to. I don't want them to punish you.'

'Don't worry about that, Mr Egozian.'

'Really, Hazel,' said the caretaker. 'If you want to apologise, I understand. Don't stop yourself because of me. Please don't do that.'

'Oh, I'm used to getting punished,' said Hazel. 'If you want someone who'd worry about a punishment, take my friend I was telling you about, the Yak. The Yak's *never* been punished. Can you imagine that? If they said they were going to punish him, it would probably scare him to death. But when someone's had as many punishments as *I've* had, one more or less doesn't matter. Once they stopped me from going on a trip in a hot-air balloon. I can't remember what I did. Yes I can! But you don't want to hear about that. Everyone else went, but guess what happened. The hot-air balloon developed a leak, and no one got to go in it! Then they decided to try again a few weeks later, but by then everyone had forgotten about my punishment, so I went as well, and I got to fly in the end. And you know what, Mr Egozian? I bet even if I *hadn't* gone that time, I would have got to fly another time anyway, so who cares? Let them give me a punishment, I'm not worried!' Hazel paused. She frowned. 'I just wish they'd tell me. It's been a week now. When are they going to decide? It's much better once you—'

'They have decided,' said Mr Egozian.

Hazel stared at him. 'Have they?' she whispered.

Mr Egozian nodded. 'I heard Mr Lamberto talking to Mrs Driscoll.' The caretaker hesitated. 'You're not going to be invited to the Frengels' celebration.'

'Not invited . . . ?'

'That's why I'm saying, Hazel, you should apologise.'

'But I can't apologise.' The words came out softly, almost as if Hazel wished they wouldn't. 'It's . . . a matter of principle.'

Mr Egozian sighed. 'If you don't apologise to Mr Davis, they won't let you go.'

15

At 9.30 sharp on Saturday morning, one week before the Frengels' party, Mrs Driscoll closed the door in the accounts room at the back of the delicatessen. She turned around. On one side of the room, six piles of crisp white envelopes stood on the desk. On the other side of the room stood five children.

Five children. Mrs Driscoll cast her eye over them. Five. *Five* children and there should have been six.

Mrs Driscoll pursed her lips. She shook her head without saying a word. The children watched her apprehensively. She glanced at her watch. She waited for a minute to pass. One minute was as much as Mrs Driscoll ever allowed. That was one of the things she'd learned as an organiser. Give people more than a minute, and they'll take an hour.

The minute was over. Mrs Driscoll gave a disapproving cough. The children glanced at each other nervously.

'Children,' said Mrs Driscoll. 'In a moment I'm going to give you the invitations to the Frengels' party. Before I do that, I will give you instructions. I will tell you exactly how to deliver the invitations, and when you are to report back to me. You will listen very carefully—'

There was a knock at the door. Mrs Driscoll stopped. Slowly, very cautiously, the door opened behind her.

Mrs Driscoll turned around. A boy was standing there, and just behind him was Mr Frengel.

'Mrs Driscoll,' said the delicatesser, 'Marcus was late.'

Mrs Driscoll lowered her nose and looked at the boy. He had red, shiny cheeks, as if he had just come in out of the snow, and spectacles with gold frames. Behind his spectacles, his eyes gazed at her with trepidation. That was something, anyway. At least the boy was scared!

'I know he's late, Mr Frengel,' said Mrs Driscoll after she had examined the boy long and hard, 'I hardly need you to tell me that. I knew it a minute and a half before he arrived.'

'But he's here now,' said the delicatesser hesitantly.

'I know he's here now, Mr Frengel. I can see that perfectly well.' Mrs Driscoll stopped, and waited to see if the delicatesser was going to say anything else.

'Um . . . He was only five minutes late.' Mr Frengel had always been intimidated by Mrs Driscoll, even before she started organising his party. After a month of having her march through his shop and call him into the accounts room for conferences, he was even more intimidated by her.

'Not five minutes, Mr Frengel,' said Mrs Driscoll, glancing at her watch ostentatiously. 'One and a half minutes late.' Being one and a half minutes late, anyone might have thought, was better than being five minutes late, but the way Mrs Driscoll said it, it sounded as if it were worse!

Mr Frengel didn't know what else to say. He stood in the doorway of his own accounts room, not daring to go inside. Marcus didn't know what to say either, and even if he had known, he probably wouldn't have had the courage to say it.

Mrs Driscoll shook her head. She sighed, as if it were a very difficult thing that she was about to do, very difficult, and very doubtful, and perhaps very *dangerous* as well.

'Come in, Marcus. Quickly! Find yourself a place.'

Marcus hesitated. Mr Frengel nudged him. He went inside. Marcus didn't know what Mrs Driscoll meant by a *place*. Everyone was squeezed together in the cramped little accounts room.

'You realise, of course, Mr Frengel,' said Mrs Driscoll, 'I'll have to start all over again now!' And with that she closed the door in the delicatesser's face.

She turned to the children again. At that moment, most of them wished they were outside as well, with Mr Frengel.

'Well, now that everyone's here . . .' she began, glancing meaningfully at Marcus, and pausing, so that everyone could glance at him as well, 'I am going to give you the instructions I *began* to give you before. You will listen very carefully to everything I say, because I rarely repeat myself. First, look at the desk. Do you see how many piles of invitations there are? Six. That's because there are six of you. As you know, there were originally supposed to be seven of you. You were each going to deliver fourteen invitations. But we all know that one particular person isn't allowed to come to the party, so she won't be delivering invitations either. That means that each of you will have to deliver sixteen invitations, and two of you will have to deliver seventeen. Is that clear? I don't want any complaints. I don't want to hear that anyone's jealous because they only get sixteen and someone else gets seventeen, and I don't want to hear that anyone thinks seventeen's too much when some people only have to deliver sixteen. If anyone's got a complaint, they can tell me now and then they can go. We don't need complainers.' Mrs Driscoll paused. 'Does anyone want to complain?' She looked at each child in turn. Not one of them would have dared to speak, even if they had wanted to. 'All right. You're very sensible children. Second,' said Mrs Driscoll, holding up a piece of paper in front of them. 'This is a list. It tells me who is delivering each invitation. *Each* one. If a single one of the invitations goes astray, I will know who failed to deliver it. Is that clear? I wouldn't want to be that person when I find out. Would you?'

The children shook their heads. They wouldn't want to be that person. They weren't even sure they wanted to be who they actually were, with Mrs Driscoll glaring at them like that.

Mrs Driscoll nodded. Then she told them she wanted the invitations delivered as soon as they left the delicatessen, and she gave them instructions about how they were to do it, and she informed them that they were to report back to her at four o'clock in the afternoon, because she was much too busy to have them coming back reporting to her whenever they felt like it. And she asked if there were any complainers again, but there weren't, so finally she called on them to take their envelopes, and one after the other the children stepped forward, in alphabetical order according to their surname, which is how Mrs Driscoll called them: Paul Boone, Marcus Bunn, Leon Davis, Mandy Furstow, Hamish Rae and Maurice Tobbler. Hazel Green, of course, would have come between Mandy Furstow and Hamish Rae, but she didn't, because she wasn't there.

Outside the delicatessen, Leon Davis poked Marcus in the ribs.

'Where were you, Marcus? You almost got us all in trouble. I bet you were with Hazel, weren't you? I bet she was *crying* because she can't come.'

Paul Boone and Hamish Rae sniggered.

'She wasn't crying!'

'I bet she was.'

'She's going to miss everything,' added Hamish cruelly, 'even the turtle eggs.'

Everyone looked at Hamish.

'Turtle eggs?' said Cobbler.

'Of course,' said Hamish, 'haven't you heard? There are going to be turtle eggs from China. Everyone's going to get two.'

Leon Davis looked at Hamish suspiciously. Turtle eggs? From China? But Leon didn't say anything out loud, because Hamish was one of his best supporters, even though he was always making up delicacies that the Frengels were supposedly going to provide.

'Who told you?' demanded Mandy Furstow.

'Doesn't matter who told him!' said Leon Davis.

'Yes, it does,' said Mandy.

Leon Davis shook his head. 'I'm going,' he said.

'I'll come with you,' said Hamish.

'So will I,' said Paul Boone.

'No. I'm going to deliver my envelopes later,' said Leon.

'But Mrs Driscoll said we have to do them now!'

'I can't do them now. We don't need to report back until four o'clock. I've got other things to do.'

'What?' said Hamish.

'I've got . . . there's a special football practice,' said Leon.

Paul frowned. 'I haven't heard about a special football practice.'

Leon shrugged. 'That's because you're not invited. Only the best player from each school has been asked.' He looked at his watch. 'I've got to go!' And before anyone could ask him anything else, he walked quickly away.

Hamish and Paul looked at each other. Then they began to follow him, slowly, from a distance, like two lost puppies who could hardly believe their master had left them behind.

Cobbler scratched his head. 'What do you think? Turtle eggs? Do turtles lay eggs? I thought it was only chickens that laid eggs.'

'Cobbler!' said Mandy Furstow. 'Ducks lay eggs. Crocodiles do as well.'

'Really?' Cobbler scratched his head again. 'Crocodiles?'

'They do, don't they, Marcus?' said Mandy.

Marcus didn't reply to that. 'Who's got the Greens' invitation?' he demanded suddenly.

'Why?' said Mandy.

'Have we got it?' demanded Marcus. He began to look through his envelopes. After a moment, the other two began as well.

'Here it is!' said Cobbler.

'Let me see.'

Cobbler held it out. But Mandy snatched it away before Marcus could take it.

'What is it, Marcus? Why do you want the Greens' invitation?'

'I've got an idea.'

'What idea?'

'Listen,' he said, and he moved closer to Mandy and Cobbler, and started whispering. 'We could open that envelope. If you use steam, you can open an envelope and no one even knows.'

'Is that true?' said Cobbler.

'I think so,' said Mandy. She gazed closely at Marcus, whispering as well. 'Why would we want to steam it open?'

'Because then we could add Hazel's name to the invitation. We could write it in. And then, next week, she could come to the party, and no one would be able to stop her.'

Mandy rolled her eyes. 'Don't you think, Marcus, someone might realise what had happened?'

'Her name would be on the invitation.'

'But everyone knows she isn't invited.'

'But she *would* be invited! Her name would be on the invitation.'

'But everyone would know someone had faked it.'

'They wouldn't.'

'They would.'

'They wouldn't.'

'They would. Mrs Driscoll wrote the invitations herself. She'd know someone had changed it. And she'd look at her list. And she'd know who delivered it!'

Marcus and Mandy looked at Cobbler.

Cobbler was scratching his head. 'I still can't work out how the steam opens the envelope.'

'Don't worry,' said Mandy, and she handed him back the Greens' envelope.

'But I'd like to know,' said Cobbler.

'Another time. Right, Marcus?'

Marcus bit his lip. 'It's so unfair. It's so unfair that they're doing this to her.'

Mandy sighed. 'If she wants to go, she just has to apologise. Why is that so hard?'

'They're picking on her,' said Marcus. 'Everyone else is invited, no matter what they've done. What about Robert Fischer? He broke Mr Petrusca's window last month when he crashed into it on his bike. Remember? But are they stopping him? *Noooo*. Only Hazel. She's the only one.'

'Actually, that's not right,' said Mandy. 'Mr Egozian isn't going either.'

Cobbler scratched his head. 'Why not? He always comes to the summer picnics.'

'Not any more,' said Mandy. 'According to the Committee, he shouldn't have been going to those either. The caretaker isn't part of the Moodey Building, he's its employee. And you don't invite your employees to your party.'

'Yes, you do!' retorted Marcus. 'My father always invites his employees to our parties.'

'Your father's only got one employee.'

'So? He invites him!'

Mandy shrugged. 'There's nothing anyone can do about it, Marcus. It's the new policy.'

'What do you mean, the new policy?'

Mandy started walking towards the entrance of the Moodey Building. 'Come on, let's deliver the invitations.'

'I don't see why Mrs Driscoll had to be so nasty about it,' muttered Marcus as he followed Mandy. 'Just because Hazel can't go to the party, it doesn't mean she can't deliver the invitations.'

'She probably wouldn't want to,' said Mandy. 'Would you?'

'I don't think I would,' said Cobbler, considering it seriously.

'Well, someone could have asked her, instead of just assuming she wouldn't.'

'You can ask her yourself, Marcus.'

They stopped. Hazel had just come out of the Moodey Building and was heading straight towards them.

16

Hazel didn't care whether she delivered the invitations or not. It was the party itself she was going to miss! What difference did the invitations make in comparison with that? She went with Marcus as he delivered his batch. Afterwards they were halfway to the delicatessen when he remembered that he wasn't supposed to report back to Mrs Driscoll before four o'clock in the afternoon. Marcus didn't think she would be very happy if anyone turned up early. Turning up early, to Mrs Driscoll, was probably as bad as turning up late.

'I can't believe she wants you to report back at all,' said Hazel. 'What for?'

Marcus shrugged. 'I don't know. She didn't explain.'

'Didn't you ask?'

Marcus stopped. 'You don't know Mrs Driscoll, Hazel. When Mrs Driscoll says something, you don't ask.'

'*I'd* ask.'

'No, I don't think even you'd ask.'

Really? Hazel raised an eyebrow. Marcus nodded. Whatever had happened in the delicatessen that morning when Mrs Driscoll handed out the invitations, it was something Marcus obviously wasn't going to forget in a hurry!

'I just don't think she trusts you,' said Hazel.

'I don't think Mrs Driscoll trusts anyone,' replied Marcus.

They started walking again, without heading any-where in particular. At the Vienna Café, on the corner of the Moodey Building, one of the waiters, Andre, came out carrying a tray of coffees with one hand. He waved to them with the other, wiggling his fingers like the tentacles of an octopus. Andre had fast hands and he could do magic tricks with cards and knew how to juggle. Once when there was no one looking he juggled four glasses for Hazel and then he added a fifth one and broke the lot. That made him laugh. 'Run!' he cried, 'Run!' When Mr Breck, the owner of the Vienna, came out to see what had happened, Andre pointed at Hazel racing away up the street and said that she had run into him and knocked the glasses out of his hand. Andre knew that Mr Breck was short-sighted, even with his glasses on, and wouldn't be able to see who was running away. And of course Andre said that all children looked the same to him as well, especially when one had just bumped into him and he hadn't got more than the quickest glance at her face.

'What are you up to, Hazel?' Andre called out, before he went back into the café.

Hazel shrugged. She looked at Marcus. 'What *are* we up to?'

Marcus shrugged as well.

Hazel frowned. Further along, through the window of Mrs Steene's art supplies shop, she could see Mrs Steene holding up a large sheet of yellow paper in front of a customer. While she was holding it, Mrs Steene glanced out at the street. She looked away quickly, pretending she hadn't seen Hazel standing there. She smiled sweetly at her customer and began to say something. Hazel could just imagine her tone of voice. Mrs Steene had a special, sticky tone of voice she used for customers, and a special, sharp one she used for other people. Hazel had never thought much of Mrs Steene, even before she came up to her apartment with Mr Davis and Mr Lamberto. There was a sign in her store saying ONLY ONE SCHOOL CHILD AT A TIME IN THE SHOP, as if a SCHOOL CHILD were some kind of dangerous animal that had to be avoided or at least carefully controlled.

Mrs Steene went to the counter to roll up the yellow piece of paper. The customer began looking at paint brushes.

Suddenly Hazel thought of something to do. 'Marcus, let's go to the art auctions.'

There were two art auctions to choose from. Mrs Gluck had mentioned them a few times, because she used to have a customer who was an art collector and sometimes bought things at the auctions. One of the auction houses was called Motheby's and the other was Mistie's, and they were opposite each other in the very same street, which was called Bunknall Row. Hazel knew where they were, because she had once been to Bunknall Row to find them. All the other shops in Bunknall Row turned out to be occupied by dealers trying to sell pieces of art to people who couldn't find anything at the auctions. Some shops had sculptures, and some had ancient pieces of pottery, and some had paintings. Hazel didn't know what made one piece of old pottery a work of art, so that it belonged in a shop in Bunknall Row, and another piece an antique, so it belonged in the Rum Warehouse, which was the big antiques market elsewhere in the city. Sometimes she suspected that no one really knew, even if they pretended they did. And as for some of the paintings, you could spend half an hour peering at one of them through the window of a shop and still not be able to make out a face or a body or what the picture was meant to be about at all.

Of course, it was only through their windows that Hazel had seen the shops in Bunknall Row. The shopkeepers *there* didn't need signs to show they didn't want children inside. The only way you'd get into one of those shops would be if an adult took you. Motheby's and Mistie's probably wouldn't want unaccompanied children either. But there must be lots of people at auctions, so it would be much harder, Hazel thought, for people to tell whether you were actually accompanied, or whether you just happened to be standing next to someone you'd never even met before. That's what she imagined, anyway, because there were no auctions actually taking place on the day she had been to Bunknall Row, so she didn't know for certain.

'You've done this before, haven't you, Hazel?' asked Marcus.

'Been to Bunknall Row? Of course, Marcus. You'll love it.'

'And you're sure we're allowed to go to the auctions?'

Allowed to go to? Hazel stopped and looked at Marcus with interest. Who was supposed to *allow* them? Marcus always assumed he couldn't do a particular thing unless some adult told him he was allowed to do it. Hazel, on the other hand, preferred to assume she could do something until someone said she *wasn't* allowed to. And even that didn't always stop her. Adults, she knew, are much too fond of telling children what they aren't allowed to do, even when it has nothing to do with them.

'Aren't you interested in seeing an art auction?' she said.

'I've never thought about it,' said Marcus.

'Then think about it now.'

They walked down Park Street in the direction of the Botanical Gardens. It would take them at least half an hour to reach Bunknall Row, perhaps longer. Hazel glanced at Marcus. He really was thinking. Maybe he'd say he wasn't interested in going after all. Marcus was like that. He was quite capable of turning around and going home if he thought he wasn't allowed to do something, even if it meant missing out on something completely new. But he rarely turned around and went home when he was with Hazel.

'I suppose you've been to the art auctions with the Yak,' he muttered eventually.

'I haven't been with the Yak,' said Hazel. 'Do you think the Yak would be interested in an art auction?'

'I don't know what he'd be interested in,' said Marcus grudgingly.

'Exactly.'

They reached the Botanical Gardens and walked beside its high brick wall.

'What *is* the Yak interested in?' said Marcus after a while, in a nonchalant tone, as if he didn't really care but it was as good a topic of conversation as any.

'Mathematics,' said Hazel.

'I see,' said Marcus.

'I doubt it. It's not like the mathematics you understand, Marcus. It's a different mathematics altogether. It's much more complicated.'

'Do you understand it?' said Marcus.

'Sometimes.' She understood it for about a second, if she was lucky.

Marcus nodded miserably.

'I'm glad you fought with him, anyway,' said Marcus. His face brightened up. 'It's about time you did. Who cares about *mathematics*?'

Hazel didn't even bother to reply to that. By now, Marcus knew perfectly well that she hadn't really fought with the Yak. Everyone knew it.

They passed the large iron gate of the gardens. Then the wall started again, and finally it ended when they came to a corner. They waited to cross the intersection, and then they continued along Park Street. In this section of Park Street, there weren't any apartment blocks, but tall brick houses standing in a long line, side by side.

'Hazel,' said Marcus.

Hazel glanced at him.

'Are you really upset about not going to the party? I mean, are you really, really upset?'

Hazel bit her lip. 'I'd like to go,' she said.

Marcus nodded. Then he shook his head. 'It's so unfair. It's *so* unfair!'

Hazel agreed, but she didn't know if she needed Marcus Bunn to keep reminding her. She wanted to go to the party. She really, really wanted to go, as Marcus might say. The people on the Committee knew what they were doing when they thought up that punishment! They couldn't have chosen anything worse. The Frengels had found special foods from all over the world for their party, as everyone knew, and there might never be another chance to taste them. Or to taste them all in one place, at one time, anyway. And no one loved discovering and trying new things as much as Hazel did, so it was a much worse punishment for her than it would have been for anyone else. Just look at Marcus. Marcus, for example, could do the same old things for a year on end and still be satisfied. He'd hardly even notice if they didn't let him go. For him, it would barely be a punishment at all. But for her . . . for her . . .

No, she thought, glancing at Marcus. That wasn't fair. It would be a punishment for Marcus as well. He had a right to go. But so did she!

'What are you thinking about, Hazel?' said Marcus.

'I was thinking about all the fun I'll have instead of going to the party,' said Hazel.

'Really?' said Marcus.

'Yes,' replied Hazel, 'it only took me quarter of a second, so then I started thinking about it all over again.'

'I tried to get them to change the invitation,' said Marcus.

'Did you? I don't think that would have worked.'

'That's what Mandy said. She said all you had to do was apologise.'

'She's right.'

'But I said you weren't going to.'

'You're right as well. ' Hazel gritted her teeth. 'It's a matter of principle.'

Marcus looked at her sympathetically. 'I suppose matters of principle are difficult, aren't they, Hazel?'

Hazel nodded. They were, she thought. They certainly were.

They waited at an intersection with a lady who was walking her dog. The dog was some kind of small terrier. When the lights changed, the terrier didn't want to move. They left the lady behind, talking to her dog, trying to convince it to start walking.

'Mr Egozian's not going either,' said Marcus suddenly.

'He's not going?'

'He's not allowed.'

'Of course he's allowed!' said Hazel. 'Don't be ridiculous, Marcus. He always goes to the summer picnics.'

'Not any more. He's an employee of the Moodey Building and employees aren't invited to parties. The Committee decided. Apparently it's the new *policy*. What does *policy* mean, Hazel?'

Hazel had stopped. 'He didn't tell me,' she murmured.

'Who didn't tell you? Was someone going to tell you what policy means?'

Hazel shook her head. 'Mr Egozian . . .'

'Mr *Egozian* was going to tell you what policy means?' demanded Marcus disbelievingly.

Hazel didn't reply. Sometimes, thought Marcus Bunn, there was just no way to understand her. He wondered whether she even understood herself. Yet he still liked her more than any other girl, more than anyone else at all, and perhaps the fact that you couldn't always understand her simply made him like her more. Marcus wished that people couldn't understand him, sometimes, but no matter how hard he tried, no one ever seemed to have any trouble knowing exactly what was going on in his mind.

Hazel was thinking. The lady with the terrier walked past them. But she didn't get more than a few paces along the pavement before the dog stopped and refused to keep going. Once again, the lady got down on her knees to persuade him to move.

Hazel sighed. 'Come on,' she said. 'Let's go to the auction.'

They started walking again.

'Have you heard the latest?' said Marcus after a while. 'The Frengels are bringing in turtle eggs. They're bringing them in from China.' Marcus clapped his hand over his mouth. 'Sorry! You don't mind me telling you, do you?'

Hazel shook her head. 'Hamish Rae's been talking again, has he?'

'It's true, Hazel. They're bringing in turtle eggs. No one would make that up. Two eggs for each person. Hazel, if they don't let you come, I'll bring you one of mine.'

'You don't need to do that, Marcus,' said Hazel. She didn't think she'd even like turtle eggs.

'I will! I'll smuggle one out. I'll put it into my pocket and I'll slip out of the courtyard very carefully when no one's looking and I'll bring it straight up—'

Marcus stopped. Hazel was looking at him.

'What?'

'That's very nice of you to say that, Marcus. It really is.'

Marcus grinned, and his cheeks, which were always rosy, went rosier than ever.

They didn't have much further to go. They came to a corner. Above them was a sign, in swirly, artistic letters, that said *Bunknall Row*. There were shops on both sides. And further along the street, opposite each other, stood two buildings that were larger than the rest.

On each of the buildings, a huge poster announced the day's sales. As Hazel and Marcus watched, latecomers hurried up the steps of the two auction houses, where proceedings were already under way.

17

Motheby's or Mistie's? Which one should they go to? According to the poster, Motheby's was auctioning EARLY PRINTS FROM THAILAND AND BURMA. Mistie's was auctioning THE COLLECTIONS OF HIS LATE EXCELLENCY THE PRINCE–MAHARAJAH OF PUTT.

'What do you think, Marcus?'

Marcus considered. 'Early prints aren't likely to be very good, are they? They probably improved later.'

'Probably.'

'And a prince–maharajah would probably be quite a good collector. He'd have a lot of money, anyway.'

'True.'

'And he *was* a late prince–maharajah, so he probably got later prints, which are better. Although it's possible he was too late to get anything.'

'When they say he's late, it means he's dead,' said Hazel.

'Really? Then how could he collect anything?'

'He probably collected things *before* he died,' said Hazel. 'It's just a guess. I could be wrong.'

'But why would he bother collecting, if he was going to die?'

Hazel opened her mouth to answer, but she stopped. It was actually a very good question, and it didn't only apply to the Prince–Maharajah. And it didn't only apply to collecting. Hazel wasn't sure there *was* any answer.

'I don't see why they can't say he's dead if he's dead,' Marcus was complaining. 'If that's what they're like, how can you believe anything they say? He might not even have been a prince–maharajah. And he might not be from Putt. And for all we know, he might not have collected *anything*!'

'Come on, Marcus,' said Hazel, and she led him towards Mistie's, even though Marcus protested that they might not even be having an auction, if you couldn't believe what was written on their poster.

Hazel and Marcus went up the steps. They found themselves in a huge entrance hall. The floor was made of green marble, and an enormous chandelier glittered and twinkled over their heads, hanging at the end of a chain from the ceiling high above them. On either side, green marble stairs led up to the first floor. And directly in front of them was an open door, through which they could see a large room. It was filled with people sitting in rows, all gazing at a man standing on a podium at the far end.

On either side of the door stood two men in smart green uniforms.

'You have done this before, haven't you?' whispered Marcus.

Hazel marched towards the door.

'Yes?' inquired one of the men as Hazel approached. The two men moved closer together, blocking the doorway. 'Yes?' said the man again. He said it softly, so as not to disturb the auction that was taking place in the room behind him, but he managed to sound stern at the same time.

Hazel didn't reply. What were you meant to say to a man who said *Yes?* What kind of a question was *Yes?* anyway?

'Can I help you?' said the man in his hushed tone.

'We're late,' said Hazel.

Marcus rolled his eyes. What was the point of telling the man they were dead? They were standing right in front of him! How much more obvious could it be that they were alive?

'Late for what?' inquired the man.

'Late for the auction,' said Hazel.

'Both of you?' said the man, and he chuckled softly, glancing at the other man beside him. The other man chuckled softly as well.

'He's later than me,' said Hazel, pointing her thumb over her shoulder at Marcus.

The man put a finger to his lips. '*Shhhh*. Run along now.'

'That's what I'm trying to do!' said Hazel.

The men chuckled again. From the room behind them, Hazel could hear the voice of the auctioneer, cold, sharp and loud, calling out numbers.

Suddenly there was a bang. The auctioneer had slapped down his gavel.

'We really are late,' said Hazel.

'Who brought you here?' whispered one of the men,

narrowing his eyes. 'You can't go in by yourself. Now, you just—'

He stopped. Hazel heard footsteps. She turned and saw a lady coming towards them across the marble floor. She was half buried in a huge fur coat and she was tottering and clattering on the highest heels Hazel had ever seen, not counting the giraffes at the zoo. Close behind her came a big man in a wide-brimmed hat and camel-coloured cloak that billowed around him as he walked.

Hazel turned back to continue the conversation. But the two guards had moved to either side of the door, and were standing very respectfully.

'Mrs van der Weygel,' said one, doffing his hat.

'Mr van der Weygel,' said the other, doffing likewise.

'I thought they'd never get here!' said Hazel, and she grabbed Marcus' hand and pulled him along with the van der Weygels before the guards could do anything to stop them.

Hazel went straight down the aisle in the middle of the room with the van der Weygels. She didn't look back. Something made her think the guards wouldn't risk creating a disturbance by coming to get her. They probably thought she'd shout and scream if they did. They were probably right. About three-quarters of the way down, there were some empty seats. The van der Weygels sat themselves right at the edge of the row.

Hazel stood there for a minute, waiting for the van der Weygels to make room.

They didn't.

'Can you move along, please?' whispered Hazel.

Mrs van der Weygel looked up. It was possible, from that look, that she had never seen a child before.

Hazel gestured with her hand for Mrs van der Weygel to move along the row. She gestured perfectly politely, she thought.

Mrs van der Weygel looked at Hazel, and shook her head, and looked at Hazel again, as if she couldn't believe that this girl was still there after all the looks she had given her. Then she turned to her husband, and tugged on his sleeve. She whispered something in his ear. Mr van der Weygel turned his head and gave Hazel an 'I've never seen a child' look, just like his wife. But once again, Hazel didn't disappear, as Mr van der Weygel was clearly expecting. Finally he raised his body and moved one seat along. Mrs van der Weygel moved with him.

'One more, please,' whispered Hazel. Obviously they hadn't noticed Marcus, who was standing behind her.

By now a number of people were watching. Hazel glanced back at the door and saw that the guards were peering in and watching as well. She smiled reassuringly. As long as the van der Weygels moved up, everything would be all right. Just as long as the van der Weygels . . . moved . . . *up* . . . The auctioneer interrupted the numbers he was calling out and coughed meaningfully. Some people were shaking their heads. Hazel knew what they'd say: it just proved children don't belong in auction houses. But it was the van der Weygels who didn't belong there if they weren't prepared to make room for other people.

Finally Mr van der Weygel moved up an extra seat. Hazel and Marcus sat down. After a moment Mrs van der Weygel looked at Hazel, turning her chin through the big soft collar of her fur coat. Then she turned back to her husband, and tugged on his sleeve, and whispered in his ear again. The van der Weygels got up and shifted another seat along.

Marcus was looking at the man on the podium. He couldn't see over the person in front of him so he had to lean one way or the other to get a glimpse. Fortunately, Hazel was sitting behind a very small old lady. She had thin, dyed brown hair gathered back in a little bun, and was smoking a cigarette in a long holder. All that Hazel could see of her was the back of her head with its bun, and her cigarette poking out on the end of its thin stick like the leg of a praying mantis. But over the top of her head, and when the cigarette wasn't waving around too much, Hazel had a good view of everything that was happening at the front of the room.

The auctioneer was standing on a podium behind a high desk. Next to him was a stand covered in red velvet. On the stand, for the moment, was a small wooden casket, studded with pearls. The auctioneer's voice raced as if he didn't have a second to waste.

three I have three three-and-a-half thank you sir four I have four four four four-and-a-half five thank you madam five five five-and-a-half sir? thank you do I hear six? do I hear six? do

I hear six? five-and-a-half against you madam do I hear six? madam do I hear six? five-and-a-half with you sir do I hear six? do I hear six? last chance ladies and gentlemen against you madam do I hear six? six? six? five-and-a-half with you sir five-and-a-half five-and-a-half five-and-a-half no more bids? five-and-a-half it is to you sir **BANG!**

The gavel came down. The casket was sold. A man in overalls came out from a door at the side of the room to take it away and a second man came out with the next thing to be sold, which was a small doll's house in dark wood.

'Five-and-a-half what?' asked Marcus, leaning across and whispering in Hazel's ear.

Hazel shrugged.

'Look at that thing,' she whispered back. 'What's a prince–maharajah doing with a doll's house?'

What would an old lady do with it? That was the next question, because soon the old lady in front of Hazel was bidding for it. She just raised her cigarette on its stick and gave it a wiggle whenever she wanted to make an offer. Every five seconds the auctioneer looked in her direction to see if the cigarette wiggled. A torrent of words and numbers poured out of his mouth.

'Hazel, he never breathes,' whispered Marcus.

'Who?'

'The man doing the auction.'

Hazel nodded. She had just been thinking the same thing. He must be able to store air in his lungs, she thought, like a whale.

His voice raced along and then **BANG!** the gavel came down again.

The old lady missed out on the doll's house. Someone else bid a higher price. Hazel felt like leaning forward to tell her that she shouldn't be upset, it was really a horrible doll's house, even if you were the kind of person who likes doll's houses, which Hazel wasn't. But suddenly the old lady looked around, and Hazel saw her profile for the first time, and she had a harsh, bird-like look in her eye, so Hazel didn't lean forward, because the old lady obviously wasn't upset at all. Which made Hazel wonder why she had bothered wiggling her cigarette in the first place.

Now there was a painting on the stand. It showed the Prince–Maharajah standing in some kind of army uniform with a white turban on his head, a rifle in one hand, and a foot balanced on the shoulder of a dead tiger. There were obviously a number of tiger-haters in the room because quite a few hands went in the air when the auctioneer asked for bids. After the dead tiger painting there was another painting. This time it showed a lake at evening with a flock of birds flying across the sky. The sky was a kind of pale yellow and the waters of the lake were a kind of yellow as well. Yet even though the colours were odd, Hazel found she liked the painting, which puzzled her.

The van der Weygels were bidding for the painting. Hazel watched them. They had their own special technique. Mr van der Weygel did the actual bidding, by raising his hat, just a fraction, off his head. Yet the auctioneer, who must have been an expert in spotting signs and signals of every type, in addition to being able to go without air for as long as a whale, had no trouble seeing it.

four do I hear five? five six? thank you madam do I hear seven?

Up went the hat.

thank you sir seven eight? thank you sir eight eight do I hear nine? thank you madam ten? ten?

Up went the hat.

thank you sir eleven? eleven? do I hear eleven? thank you sir twelve?

Up went the hat . . .

Yet while it was Mr van der Weygel's hat that went up, it was Mrs van der Weygel who told him when to lift it. They had their own technique for this as well. Mr van der Weygel was lifting his hat with his right hand. His left arm was resting on his thigh, and Mrs van der Weygel's right hand lay on his wrist. When she wanted him to bid she tapped him once. Just a single tap with her forefinger. Mr van der Weygel never even looked down. Just a single tap from his wife, and whenever he felt it, he bid. Hazel watched in fascination. Tap . . . Up went the hat. Tap . . . Up went the hat.

The price of the painting was rising steadily. Now there were only two bidders, the van der Weygels and a lady three rows in front of them.

eighteen do I hear nineteen? nineteen? nineteen? I'll take eighteen-and-a-half do I hear eighteen-and-a-half? do I hear eighteen-and-a-half? thank you madam eighteen-and-a-half

nineteen? nineteen now against you sir nineteen? do I hear
nineteen? nineteen?

Tap . . . Up went the hat.

thank you sir nineteen nineteen do I hear nineteen-and-
a-half? nineteen-and-a-half? against you madam nineteen-
and-a-half madam do I hear nineteen-and-a-half? thank
you madam twenty? do I hear twenty sir? against you sir
twenty? twenty? do I hear twenty sir? do I hear

'Hazel!' It was Marcus, whispering in her ear. 'Hazel,
look who's there!'

'Where?' said Hazel impatiently. She was more
interested in seeing what the van der Weygels would do.
'There.'

Hazel turned to look. She couldn't see who Marcus
was talking about. 'Where, Marcus?'

Marcus pointed across the room.

twenty-and-a-half to the young gentleman

Marcus froze. His eyes went wide.

'Me?'

His voice echoed through the room. For a moment
there was silence. Even the auctioneer had stopped.
Everyone in the room was looking at Marcus.

The auctioneer's voice raced off again.

twenty-and-a-half to the young gentleman twenty-and-a-
half do I hear twenty-one? sir madam do I hear twenty-one?
against you sir against you madam do I hear twenty-one?
twenty-and-a-half to the young gentleman twenty-and-a-
half twenty-and-a-half do I hear twenty-one?

'Hazel, bid!' whispered Marcus.

'Why?'

'I don't have twenty-and-a-half . . . twenty-and-a-half . . . whatever it is that I bid twenty-and-a-half of!'

'Marcus, what am I going to do with a big painting like that? I haven't got room on my wall.'

twenty-and-a-half to the young gentleman do I hear twenty-one? do I hear twenty-one? last chance ladies and gentlemen

'Hazel . . .' wailed Marcus softly.

Hazel looked along the row. On the other side of the empty seat that separated them, Mrs van der Weygel was watching her stonily.

twenty-one? twenty-one?

Hazel glanced at Mrs van der Weygel's hand. Mrs van der Weygel saw where she was looking. Her finger rose. It stayed there, hovering tantalisingly in the air.

twenty-and-a-half twenty-and-a-half twenty-and-a-half

Hazel looked up questioningly. Mrs van der Weygel held her gaze. Their eyes met.

no more bids? twenty-and-a-half it is to

The finger fell. Mr van der Weygel's hat went up.

twenty-one thank you sir you left it late sir but better late than never twenty-one twenty-one against the young gentleman, do I hear twenty-one-and-a-half? do I hear twenty-one-and-a-half?

No, not from the young gentleman. Marcus sat there as if he had been petrified, rigid, like a statue. He didn't move a muscle, he hardly dared to blink, in case he'd end up having to buy a painting of a yellow lake with money that he didn't even have.

'Who was it you wanted to show me?' whispered Hazel,

when the painting had finally been sold to the van der Weygels and the next item was being placed on the stand.

'Over there,' whispered Marcus, holding his arms tightly by his side.

'Where?'

Slowly, very, very slowly, and very slightly, Marcus turned his head towards the front corner of the room.

'There,' he said.

Hazel looked. 'Who is it?'

'The Davises.'

Hazel looked again. Marcus was right! In the second row from the front, a few seats in from the aisle, sat the Davises: Mr Davis, and Mrs Davis, and Martin, Leon's older brother, and Leon himself, sandwiched between his parents.

18

After the auction, Hazel and Marcus were amongst the first ones out. Hazel wanted to thank the guards for having let them in, but they were too busy bowing their heads and doffing their hats at other people to pay them any attention. Hazel and Marcus leaned against the wall of Motheby's, across the street, and watched everyone else come down the stairs.

'Are you all right, Marcus?' said Hazel.

Marcus nodded.

'I thought you were going to have a heart attack, you know, when you started bidding for that painting. I was really quite worried.'

'I was worried, too,' said Marcus.

'You shouldn't bid if you can't stand the suspense,' Hazel advised him.

Marcus nodded again. He didn't need Hazel to tell him that!

Hazel looked back at the people coming out of the building. She just wanted to see what Leon would do when he saw them across the street. He'd probably pretend he didn't know they were there. He'd glance across, in the sly, sideways habit people have when they don't want anyone to know they're looking. It was funny, people could never resist doing that, Hazel had noticed. They could never resist looking at the very thing they were trying to ignore.

The van der Weygels appeared at the top of the steps. Mrs van der Weygel spotted Hazel and tossed her head. She began to clatter down the steps on her high heels, clutching her husband's arm. Hazel gave her a big smile.

'Where do you think their painting is?' said Marcus.

'They must be getting it delivered later.'

'I wouldn't get it delivered later,' said Marcus. 'If *I* bought a painting like that, I'd want to take it straight home and see what it looked like on my wall.'

'But you didn't buy it, Marcus,' Hazel pointed out.

'I almost did,' muttered Marcus, who still couldn't quite believe what had happened. He shivered, thinking about it.

Hazel disagreed. Marcus didn't almost buy the painting—the painting almost sold itself to him. How something could do that to a boy—something that couldn't talk or move or do anything, and which was actually just a piece of canvas covered in paint—was an interesting puzzle, and well worth some thought.

'Perhaps Leon didn't see us,' said Marcus.

'Marcus, *everyone* saw us. Or you, anyway.'

And here came the Davises, finally, amongst the last of the crowd. First the parents appeared at the top of the steps, then Martin, who was four years older than Leon and had grown so much in the past year that he was almost as tall as his father, and then Leon himself. And they *all* gave Hazel the sideways glance of people who can't keep their eyes off the person they don't want to see.

Hazel grinned. That was better than expected!

'Hazel,' said Marcus, 'I've just remembered something.'

He frowned. 'Leon isn't meant to be here. He's meant to be at a football practice.'

'How do you know?'

'He said so. I heard him. He said he had to go to a special football practice. Only the best player in each school was invited.'

Hazel glanced at Marcus with interest. Really? Only the best player in each school? Only one? And now Leon was here. Hazel raised an eyebrow. This all sounded a little . . . fishy.

She looked back across the street. On the pavement, the crowd was thick. She couldn't see the Davises. Then she glimpsed the top of Mr Davis' head, but after a moment it disappeared around a corner.

'Supposed to be at a special football practice . . .' murmured Hazel, 'but at an art auction instead. Curious, don't you think, Marcus?'

'Yes,' said Marcus, 'it is curious.'

'Why would Leon lie about something like that? And why was he at an art auction, anyway? He hates art.'

'He does. You're right.'

'I think we should ask him,' said Hazel Green.

'When?'

'Now.'

Through the crowd, Hazel could see Leon Davis coming back towards them.

'So, Leon, you've become an *art* collector,' said Hazel, when Leon reached them. 'And there we were, all of us, thinking you were practising football with the best players from the other schools.'

'I *do* practise football with the best players from the other schools.'

'Really? That's strange. I could swear I saw you just now when they auctioned the collections of the Prince–Maharajah of Putt. You and your whole family. But it must have been some other people who looked like you. Marcus, did you see them? The Davis family look-alikes?'

Marcus nodded. 'I saw them. At the auction of the collections of the *late* Prince–Maharajah of Putt,' he added.

Leon Davis glared at him. 'At least I don't bid for things I can't afford to buy!'

'Oh, Leon! What a terrible thing to say!' cried Hazel. 'How do you know he couldn't afford to buy it? Marcus' parents are very generous. He gets a lot of pocket money, don't you, Marcus?'

Marcus stared questioningly at Hazel.

'*Don't* you, Marcus?'

Marcus nodded.

Leon Davis scoffed.

'Besides, how do you know his parents didn't send him to buy that painting? Just because *your* parents obviously don't trust you to go by yourself . . . And at least he made a bid,' added Hazel. 'I didn't see you bid, Leon Davis. Or your lookalike parents, for that matter.'

'They never bid,' muttered Leon. He leaned against the wall beside Marcus. 'They're always going to these auctions, and they're always talking about how they're going to buy this thing or that thing, but they never do.'

'Why do they go?'

Leon shrugged. 'They just do,' he said. 'And now they've started taking me as well. They say it'll be good for my education.'

'What do they want you to be when you grow up?' said Hazel. 'A professional bidder?'

Marcus laughed. Leon didn't.

'You can't believe how boring it is,' Leon said.

'Yes we can,' said Marcus. He had been bored for a good part of the auction, which had gone on for a long time, except when he was bidding, of course, when he was terrified.

'Everyone's sixty years old and you have to sit there for hours as if you're sixty as well.'

'And you can't move or the auction man will try to sell you something,' muttered Marcus.

'Everyone's always telling you to keep still,' said Leon.

'And people would laugh if they found out your parents drag you along like a baby,' added Hazel.

'I know. They really would.' Leon nodded despondently.

'Well, Leon, I think you've got a problem.'

Leon looked up sharply. 'You wouldn't *tell,* Hazel Green!'

'I wouldn't tell because . . .?'

'It wouldn't . . . it wouldn't be fair!'

Hazel shook her head. She glanced at Marcus. 'That's what he's worried about, isn't it, Marcus? That's why he came back to find us. And I thought he just came for a chat! Do you remember when Mr Petrusca's lobsters were stolen, Marcus, and I had to go to the Greville Building and carry a placard? Leon didn't mind telling people about that. Oh no, he thought everyone ought to know. But going to art auctions is much worse than carrying a placard outside the Greville Building. There's no comparison, is there?'

'None,' said Marcus.

'That's rubbish, Hazel Green!'

Hazel shrugged. As far as she could see, it didn't matter if it *was* rubbish—Leon was in no position to tell her how to dispose of it.

'Why *would* you tell, anyway?' said Leon.

Hazel smiled. She knew that trick. She had tried it lots of times herself, and was much better at it than Leon. Just look at him! He wasn't very convincing. He had folded his arms, and put his nose in the air, trying to look as if he didn't care. He looked as if he were searching for pigeons.

'Well, Robert Fischer might like to know, for example,' she explained.

'And Hamish Rae and Paul Boone,' Marcus reminded her. 'They might like to know why he isn't at football practice, after he told them that's where he was going.'

'Yes, I'm sure they would. And Sam Gunston would be interested, don't you think, Marcus? And then there's Sophie Wigg, and Nicholas Buch, and . . . Do you know what I think, Marcus? I think *everyone* would like to know.'

Leon stopped pretending and glared at her.

'Of course,' said Hazel, 'they don't *have* to know.'

Leon's eyes narrowed.

'I mean, I don't *have* to tell them.'

'What do you want, Hazel Green?' asked Leon in a low voice.

'I just want you to explain something to me.'

'What about?'

'You'll have to decide whether you're going to do it first.'

'How can I decide? I bet you're going to ask some embarrassing question and then you'll tell everyone about *that* instead.'

'No,' said Hazel. 'Not at all. I have no wish to embarrass you, Leon.' She grinned. 'Anyway, what could be more embarrassing than going to art auctions when you tell everyone you're practising football?'

'I don't go to art auctions,' said Leon through gritted teeth.

'Excuse me?'

'Hardly ever! Hardly ever at all!'

'Of course not. You're probably learning ballet the rest of the time.'

'I do *not* go to ballet,' hissed Leon Davis. 'Never! I never go to ballet! That was a long time ago! I didn't have a choice. Anyway, a lot of football players do ballet when they're young. Lots of them! My mother says so. It helps . . . it helps develop foot skills . . .' Leon's voice died away as he realised what he had been saying. 'What do you want to know?' he demanded suddenly. 'What?'

Hazel glanced at Marcus. Marcus was staring at Leon in disbelief.

'*Ballet*, Leon?' said Hazel, trying to keep the grin off her face. 'Is that what you just said?'

'See! I knew you just wanted to embarrass me. That's what you want, isn't it?'

Hazel shook her head. 'No, it isn't. Don't be worried, Leon. Do you think you're really so interesting? What I want to know isn't even about you. It's about your father.'

'My father?' Leon smirked derisively. 'You just can't bring yourself to apologise, can you?'

'No,' said Hazel, 'I'm not going to apologise. But I *am* going to tell everybody where you were today. And maybe I'll tell them about your ballet lessons as well. There's only one way to stop me doing that.'

Leon frowned. He glanced at Marcus for a second. Marcus nodded.

'All right,' said Leon eventually, 'but you'll have to swear you won't tell about me.'

'Naturally,' said Hazel. 'And you'll have to swear you'll answer my questions honestly.'

'One question! You only get one question.'

'That's all I need,' said Hazel.

'All right.'

'All right.'

Hazel put her finger on her nose. Leon touched his nose as well. They watched each other carefully. Then, at exactly the same instant, they opened their mouths to speak.

'I swear . . .'

. . .

Hazel didn't ask her question immediately. They began to walk back to the Moodey Building. Leon kept glancing at her nervously, wondering what her question was going to be. It wasn't such a bad thing, Hazel thought, for a boy like Leon to be kept in suspense occasionally.

They had reached the iron gates of the Botanical Gardens. Suddenly Hazel turned and went in. Leon and Marcus followed her.

'All right,' said Hazel, as they crunched over the gravel path that ran between the Orange House and the Moss Meadow. 'Here it is.'

Leon stopped. He looked at her seriously. Marcus waited to hear what the question was as well.

'Can't you guess what it is?' said Hazel. 'It's very simple.'

'I didn't swear that I had to guess it, Hazel. If you don't want to tell me what it is, that's fine. I won't have to answer.'

'All right, this is it. I want to know why your father hates Mr Egozian's people.'

Leon smiled sarcastically. 'That? You're still thinking about that? You just can't bring yourself to admit you lied about my father.'

'Answer the question, Leon. Why does he hate them?'

'He doesn't hate them. There! That's your answer. You've just got this crazy idea—'

Hazel turned and started walking away. Leon and Marcus ran after her.

'Hazel!'

'You swore you'd answer honestly,' Hazel said to Leon, without slackening her pace. 'Marcus, you heard him.'

'I have answered honestly.'

'You haven't. You haven't even answered the question I asked. I didn't ask you whether your father hates Mr Egozian's kind of people. I asked you why.'

'How can I answer *why* when he doesn't?'

'All right, Leon. If that's your answer, that's your answer.' Hazel turned to Marcus. 'I wonder where we can find Robert Fischer. Or perhaps we should start with Sam Gunston.'

'Sam's probably at home,' said Marcus. 'He has to babysit his sisters on Saturday afternoons.'

'Good. Well, we'll go there first. And then we'll find Hamish Rae, and after that—'

'All right! Stop! Hazel, stop!'

Hazel stopped. 'Well?' she said.

Leon bit his lip. 'I think saying he *hates* them is a bit too strong.'

'All right. Let's say he doesn't like them.'

'No,' said Leon quietly. He looked at the ground. 'He doesn't.'

Hazel sat down on a bench. She waited until Leon sat down as well.

'Why?' she asked.

19

'They were poor. Very poor.'

Leon Davis paused for a moment. He shook his head, thinking about it.

'You have no idea how poor they were, Hazel. One year, my father went to school without any shoes. He's always telling us about it. Eight years old, and he had no shoes for a whole year, summer, winter, rain and shine. And when he was in high school, he had to work at night in a salami-stuffing factory. And if he didn't get a scholarship to the university, he wouldn't be anything today. Do you think his family could have afforded it? And even when he was at university he had to keep working in the factory, while he was studying to be a lawyer, to support the family. By then his mother was sick. His father had died long before. He was the oldest and there were four other children. Who else was going to support them? Whatever my uncles and aunts have made of themselves today, it's because of him. He never lets them forget it. He worked and worked and worked. *That's* how you succeed in life, if you're going to pull yourself out of the gutter. Work. Hard work. That's what he says. All his life, when he was a boy, when he was a student, as a lawyer, he's worked and worked and worked.'

'So he's worked a lot, then?'

Leon Davis glanced at her sharply. 'Are you going to listen, Hazel, or are you going to crack jokes?'

Hazel nodded. Leon glanced at Marcus, who was watching him intently.

'People wouldn't know it today. You know what my father says? "When people look at me, what do they see? They don't see the boy who went to school for a year without any shoes. They don't see the young man who stuffed salamis until midnight for seven years of his life. They see Julius Davis, a wealthy, successful lawyer. Julius Davis. And that's how it should be!"' Leon sighed. 'That's why he wants me to have everything. That's why he takes us to the art auctions, to see all the beautiful things in the world. When he was a boy, he never saw anything, not a painting, not a clock. All he saw was work.'

And his socks, thought Hazel, when he didn't have any shoes for a year. And probably his toes as well, because his socks would soon have worn out. Still, Hazel wasn't sure if all of this made complete sense. If Mr Davis thought hard work was so important, shouldn't he be sending Leon out to stuff salamis instead of dragging him along to Mistie's art auctions on Saturday mornings?

And that wasn't the only thing that puzzled her. 'What's this got to do with Mr Egozian?'

'Wait, I'm coming to that. Why do you think they were so poor? When my grandparents came to this country, they had nothing. In fact, they had less than nothing. They owed a big debt. They didn't have the money for the journey. In the village they came from there was only one rich man, and his name was Mr Tudarian. Whenever anyone needed money they had to go to him.'

'What about a bank?' said Marcus.

'Banks? There were no banks. Where would you find a bank in a place like that?'

Marcus glanced at Hazel and shrugged. Why shouldn't you be able to find a bank there?

Leon turned back to Hazel. 'Everyone knew what Mr Tudarian was like. Everyone had seen other people in the village who had been ruined, turned out of their houses into the snow, when he came to demand his interest. But there was no one else to lend them the money they needed. So they borrowed it. They were worried about how they would pay the money back, because they would be here and Mr Tudarian would still be in the village. "Don't worry," said Mr Tudarian. "I have a nephew who lives there. He'll collect it." And he did. Every week Mr Tudarian's nephew would come to their apartment, and whenever there was any money, he'd take it all as interest on the debt. But often there was no money, and however much they paid, the interest kept rising. They ended up owing much more than they had ever borrowed. And there was no mercy, Hazel. When the nephew came, he took everything. Even after my grandfather died, Tudarian's nephew kept coming, searching for his payment. If anything, it got worse. Now, when there was no money, he'd take other things, things he couldn't even use or sell, as a punishment. My father's shoes, for instance. One day there was no money for him, so Tudarian's nephew took the shoes instead. What was he going to do with the shoes of an eight-year-old child? Nothing. He threw them out the window into the river, right in front of my father's eyes. What good did it do him? Or he'd turn the furniture upside down. Sometimes he'd rip open the mattress. Once, when he found a note hidden there, Tudarian's nephew hit my grandmother in the face, to teach her she should never do such a thing again. You should hear my father tell the story. My mother doesn't like him to, but he says, no, why shouldn't the boys hear it? Can you imagine what it's like to see some stranger come into your home and hit your mother across the face? So what do you think, Hazel? Why shouldn't he hate them? Tudarian, his nephew, Egozian, all of them? Why not? No shoes for a year. Every day he'd go to school and everyone would laugh at him. Point at him. The boy whose family was so poor they couldn't even afford a pair of shoes. But he still went. If they'd done all that to you, if you'd seen them punch your mother, wouldn't you hate them too?'

Hazel thought. Maybe she would hate Tudarian. Maybe she would. And maybe she'd hate his nephew as well. It was an awful story, and if even part of it was true—allowing for the way Leon always exaggerated things—it was enough to make you hate a lot of people, unless you tried to stop yourself from hating them.

'But I still don't see what it's got to do with Mr Egozian,' she said eventually. 'He didn't hit your father's mother. Why does your father hate him?'

'Because he's the same! He comes from the same people.' Leon looked at Hazel as if he couldn't believe anyone could be so stupid. 'They're all the same. All they care about is money. Isn't it obvious? Egozian doesn't have the chance to do that kind of thing, that's all. Now the boot's on the other foot! But Egozian would do it if he could.'

'Is that what your father says?' asked Hazel.

Leon didn't answer that. 'It's just how those people are, Hazel. No one's blaming them. It's not their *fault*. They can't help it. You've just got to make sure you never have anything to do with them. Whatever they want to do to each other, that's fine. Just keep them away from everybody else.'

Hazel couldn't believe what she was hearing. But Leon was staring straight back at her, without the slightest sign of embarrassment at all the rubbish he'd just said.

'Do you really think Mr Egozian would hit your grandmother?' said Hazel eventually. She wasn't sure if she was angry at Leon, for saying such ridiculous things, or sorry for him, for believing them. She glanced at Marcus for a second, and shook her head. Marcus shrugged. Hazel turned back to Leon. 'Do you really think so, Leon? Mr Egozian? Do you really think he'd throw away your shoes just to make you suffer for a year?'

Leon smiled smugly. 'He's never had the chance,' he said.

Hazel felt like punching Leon in the nose, just to let him see what *she* could do when she had the chance.

She drew a deep breath. 'Leon Davis,' she said, 'how many Davises are there in the world? Do you think I dislike all of them just because of you? Do you think

I don't realise there are probably some very decent Davises around, some quite intelligent ones, even some pleasant ones—although I've never actually *met* one!'

'Very funny,' said Leon. He got up. 'I've answered your question. I don't have to say anything else. Be friends with Mr Egozian, if you like. See if I care. Just watch out for your money—that's all he's after!'

Leon walked away.

'I don't understand this at all,' murmured Marcus Bunn, as Leon went out of the gate and disappeared. 'Mr Egozian doesn't *have* any money. Not unless he hides it away and never spends it on anything.'

Hazel glanced at him. 'Marcus . . .' she said, but she didn't go on.

There was so much to think about. Hazel wasn't sure how to put it all together. On the one hand, what about the story Mr Egozian had told her, the way his people had once been slaughtered like sheep? On the other hand, what about this Mr Tudarian, who seemed like the nastiest character you could imagine—apart from his nephew, who was even nastier. And on the third hand, there was Mr Egozian himself, who was gentle, honest and kind. Where did he fit in? And on the fourth hand, there was this ridiculous idea of hating a whole people— a whole people—just because one or two of them had treated you badly!

Hazel didn't have enough hands. That was the problem. You had to juggle these ideas, and juggling them meant you could never get hold of them all at the same time.

Marcus waited. Eventually Hazel stood up and they headed back to the Moodey Building. Hazel didn't feel very talkative. Marcus glanced at her now and then, wondering what she was thinking about.

'Hazel,' he said eventually, 'is it really such an embarrassing thing to go to art auctions?'

Hazel shrugged. 'Leon seems to think so.'

'It's just . . . I don't think it's so embarrassing. I mean, it is a bit boring, but I don't see what's so embarrassing about it. And if it is so embarrassing, when we said we were going to tell all his friends, Leon could easily have said *he* was going to tell all *our* friends that we were there as well. That should have stopped us, shouldn't it? If it really is so embarrassing, I mean.'

'But that wouldn't have worked,' said Hazel. 'And Leon knew it, didn't he?'

Marcus nodded. Apparently Leon did know it, but Marcus still didn't understand how.

'Besides, Leon lied when he said where he was going. He was never going to a football practice at all. Maybe that's what he was really frightened of, that everyone would find out he lied.'

'But he's lied before,' said Marcus.

Hazel smiled. That was true!

Marcus sighed. 'Well, I don't think I would have done what he did. I don't think I would have agreed to tell about my father.'

'No,' said Hazel.

'You didn't tell about Mr Petrusca that time, did you,

after everyone heard about the placard you were carrying?'

Hazel shook her head.

'I remember. You had to be silent. You couldn't tell them why you were carrying it, even when they made fun of you.'

'No, I couldn't tell them why.'

Marcus frowned. 'It's like betraying him. It's like he betrayed his own father.'

'Well, that's Leon,' said Hazel. 'He doesn't want everyone to laugh at him. He probably doesn't realise I laugh at him all the time, anyway.'

Marcus grinned. 'Do you know what, Hazel?' he said suddenly. 'I've just thought of something. I didn't swear, did I? I didn't swear I wouldn't say where Leon was today.'

'No, you didn't.'

'So *I* could tell. I could tell all his friends if we wanted to.'

20

'I've heard there are going to be turtle eggs,' said Mrs Gluck, putting together a bouquet of yellow rosebuds with honey-coloured carnations.

'I've heard that as well,' said Hazel.

'I'm not sure if I really want to eat turtle eggs,' said Mrs Gluck.

'You won't *have* to, Mrs Gluck. They can't make you eat them.'

Mrs Gluck chuckled. 'That's true.'

'Mr Volio told me he's going to make pastries with a special marzipan you can only get in Italy. He told the Frengels where it comes from and they ordered it for him. It arrived yesterday.'

'That should be nice,' said Mrs Gluck.

'You don't sound very excited,' said Hazel. People who had the chance to go to the party could at least sound excited about it! 'Aren't you looking forward to it, Mrs Gluck?'

'Of course I am, Hazel.' The florist twisted a length of twine around the stems of the bouquet she had just made. Her hands moved so fast that the twine whirled in a blur. She got up and put the bouquet in a vase. 'It'll be a lot of work, though. I'll be up at four o'clock on Saturday morning to get the flowers ready. Mrs Driscoll is being very particular. She wants irises and tulips on every table, irises and lilies on the walls, and irises, tulips *and* lilies on the head table.'

'What do the Frengels want?' said Hazel.

'I'm not sure Mrs Driscoll bothered to ask them.'

Hazel smiled. Mrs Gluck began working on her next arrangement.

'Mr Volio said he'd give me one of the pastries,' said Hazel. 'He said no one would notice if there was one less.'

Mrs Gluck glanced at Hazel. 'I'm sure he's right,' she said.

Hazel nodded. She sighed, and leaned forward on the worktable with her chin on her hands. Mrs Gluck watched her for a moment before she turned back to her arrangement.

It was quite a complicated arrangement, with two speckled lilies as the centrepiece and a selection of tulips and small chrysanthemums around them. Mrs Gluck tried a couple of variations and even thought of adding one or two irises. From time to time she glanced at Hazel. Hazel was just staring, staring at the worktable, which was covered in leaves that Mrs Gluck had plucked off the stems of earlier arrangements.

It was strange, suddenly Hazel found herself feeling quite glum, gazing at all those leaves. She had never felt glum at the leaves on Mrs Gluck's worktable before. But they were being discarded, when you thought about it, as if they weren't good enough, or were too ugly, to be part of the arrangements. And yet it wasn't their fault they were leaves. What could they do about it? No, being a leaf, apparently, meant that you were fated to be thrown away. But what if *they* were the flowers, and the flowers that Mrs Gluck had just put in her arrangements were the leaves? Then the boot would be on the other foot! And if the boot was on the other foot, well . . . those leaves would be a lot happier, Hazel thought, because for a start, they wouldn't be leaves at all, but flowers, and for a finish, they'd have a boot, and it must be better to have a boot, even if you were a leaf, than no boots at all, even if you were a flower. But the leaves *would* be flowers, wouldn't they? And there couldn't be many flowers that had boots, in fact, it must be a very rare thing, very rare indeed, and very . . . very . . . *strange* . . .

'Hazel?'

Hazel looked up.

'What are you thinking about?'

Hazel shook her head. 'I don't know, Mrs Gluck.'

'Don't know or won't say?'

'Don't know. I'm serious, Mrs Gluck. I've got no idea.'

Mrs Gluck raised an eyebrow.

'Doesn't it ever happen to you, Mrs Gluck, that you start thinking about something, and at the start it seems perfectly normal, and by the end of it you've got to a completely different idea that seems very strange, if not ridiculous?'

'No,' said Mrs Gluck. 'Very rarely, if ever.'

'I suppose that's a good thing,' said Hazel, but she wasn't *sure* it was a good thing, because she liked ridiculous ideas, and she often had to make them up herself, since other people rarely did it for her.

Mrs Gluck was still watching her. Eventually she shook her head. 'Sometimes, Hazel Green, I don't understand you at all.'

Hazel smiled. Who wanted to be understood all the time?

Mrs Gluck went on to her next arrangement. She was starting with daffodils and red gerberas. Mrs Gluck didn't often use daffodils, which she thought were the least interesting flower of all, but even the least interesting flower of all was sometimes the right flower to use, and in those cases Mrs Gluck was prepared to use it.

'Weren't you going to try to get proof?' said Mrs Gluck suddenly.

'Proof?'

'I thought perhaps that's what you were thinking about.'

'Oh,' said Hazel. 'No, there is no proof, Mrs Gluck. Mr Egozian won't speak. And there's no one else.'

'If he won't speak, he won't speak. You can't force him.'

'I know I can't force him. I haven't even tried to force him. I have got the motive, though.'

'What is it?'

'I can't say,' said Hazel.

Mrs Gluck peered at Hazel closely.

Hazel bit her lip. The more she thought about it, the

less proud she was of the way she had made Leon Davis speak. It was a kind of blackmail that she had used, she thought, threatening to tell where he had been after he had deceived his friends. And if you shouldn't lie to defend the truth, which was why she hadn't asked the Yak to pretend to be a witness, blackmailing someone wasn't much better.

Mrs Gluck sighed. 'Well, the motive's not enough. I used to have a customer once, Hazel. His name was Mr O'Riordan. And he used to say—'

'Don't worry about a motive—get proof!'

Mrs Gluck frowned. 'Exactly,' she murmured.

'Well, I don't have proof,' said Hazel. 'I just don't have it. I know *what* Mr Davis did, and I know *why* he did it. But I can't prove it.'

Mrs Gluck stopped working on the arrangement. She gazed very seriously at Hazel. 'And you're still not going to apologise, are you?'

Hazel didn't even answer that.

Mrs Gluck nodded. She gazed at Hazel, as if trying to make her mind up about something. Suddenly Mrs Gluck put the arrangement down. It was only half finished, and it was almost unheard of for Mrs Gluck to stop in the middle of an arrangement. But now she put the flowers down, sat back on her high working chair, and folded her arms.

'Hazel, I'm going to tell you a story.'

'You already told me about Mr O'Riordan, Mrs Gluck. I know, it's not the motive you have to worry about, it's—'

'No, another story, Hazel. Just listen.' Mrs Gluck

paused. 'This is a story about someone called Mrs Viner. Have you ever heard of Mrs Viner, Hazel?'

Hazel shook her head.

Mrs Gluck chuckled. 'There was a time when *everyone* had heard of Mrs Viner. This was long ago, Hazel, before you were born. It was when the MacKenzie brothers were building the Sage Centre. You've probably never heard of the MacKenzie brothers, either, but around this time they were just about the richest men in the city. They were builders, and the Sage Centre was their finest development. Originally, it was called the MacKenzie Centre. You didn't know that either, did you?'

Hazel shook her head.

'Well, it isn't called the MacKenzie Centre any more, and I'll tell you why. That building stands on land where there used to be some very old houses, probably the oldest houses in the city. You know the two houses in Bentmore Square? They were just like them. Thanks to the MacKenzies and the other developers, the ones in Bentmore Square are just about the only ones left now. But even back then, a few people were starting to say we should preserve our history better. Mrs Viner was one of them. So when the MacKenzie brothers started buying up those old houses just so they could knock them down and build their centre, she fought them every step of the way. Every time the council met, there she was at the head of the protesters, trying to make sure the council didn't give permission. Every time the MacKenzies put in a submission, she put in another one against them. Just save a few of the houses, she demanded, just three or four. Build around them. But that didn't fit in with the MacKenzies' plans. She started petitions. She got the newspapers to write stories. Oh, the MacKenzie boys used every trick in the book, of course. They offered her money. She refused it. They threatened her. She ignored them. Eventually the council gave permission for them to go ahead—half the councillors had been bribed by the MacKenzies anyway. The protesters gave up. The tenants moved out of the houses. Only Mrs Viner refused to quit. The day came for the demolition to begin. The wreckers arrived. But imagine, Hazel, just before they were about to start the demolition, what do you think they saw?'

'*Mrs Gluck!*'

Mrs Gluck and Hazel looked around. Sophie was standing in the doorway.

'Mrs Gluck, I just sold the last zinnias!'

'There's some more over there. Take them in, Sophie.'

Sophie stood and stared.

'I'm busy. Take them in, Sophie.'

Sophie walked *slowly* around the table. Hazel watched her. Sophie picked up the flowers and walked *slowly* out of the workroom.

'Now, where was I?' said Mrs Gluck.

Hazel turned back to her. 'The wreckers saw something just before they started the demolition.'

'That's right. This is the best part of the story! Just before they were about to start, the wreckers looked up and saw Mrs Viner, sitting in the window of one of the attics, waving at them.'

Hazel laughed.

'That's right, just sitting there, waving.'

'How did she get in?'

'No one knows. Perhaps she found a burglar to help her. There was never a more resourceful woman than Mrs Viner. Anyway, the MacKenzies told the wreckers to ignore her, but they wouldn't touch the place. They weren't going to be responsible for injuring a defenceless old lady. One of them went up to ask her to come out, but she said she wasn't coming unless they dragged her out. The MacKenzies told them to do it, but they refused. They were wreckers, not draggers! So the MacKenzies got the police, and two of the officers went up and told her it was illegal for her to be there, because it was the MacKenzies' property, and they'd have to arrest her if she didn't leave. Well, then they'd have to arrest her, said Mrs Viner, but before they did it they ought to realise that she was squatting. And as soon as she said the word *squatting*, the police turned around and went down to tell the MacKenzies that they'd have to go to a judge, and get a special order to evict her, because squatters have certain rights once they get into empty buildings and you can't just arrest them. And the judge might want to hold a hearing, and it might take days, or even weeks, until he gave the order. And in the meantime there were fifty wreckers, all waiting to get to work, and the MacKenzies had to pay them for every hour they were there.'

'So what happened?'

'Well, the wreckers were standing around, the police had gone off to find a judge, and . . . the MacKenzie boys went inside themselves! They had started off as bricklayers, so they were big boys, Hazel, and old Mrs Viner didn't stand a chance. Up they went, and five minutes later down they came, carrying her head and foot. They threw her on the pavement and told the wreckers to get to work.'

'And *then* what happened? The wreckers refused to work, didn't they?'

'No. They went right ahead.'

'But the council stopped the building?'

'No, the Centre was finished a year later, right on schedule.'

'I don't understand, Mrs Gluck.'

'Listen, Hazel. Mrs Viner knew she was going to be thrown out. She had actually expected the wreckers to do it, and no one was more surprised than her when they refused. In fact, to be thrown out was exactly what she *wanted*. She wanted the city to see it, to see how she was dragged down and tossed away, which, in a way, was what was being done to our history. It was the last protest she could make. And she was a woman who knew how to make a protest!' Mrs Gluck chuckled. 'She'd tipped off photographers from every newspaper in the city. They were hiding in the alleyways all around, just waiting for the right moment.'

Hazel smiled, beginning to understand.

Mrs Gluck smiled as well. 'It was the biggest mistake

the MacKenzies ever made. Mrs Viner couldn't have dreamed they'd do it themselves. Neither could the photographers. When the MacKenzies came down those stairs, a whole crowd of photographers stepped out of the alleys to surprise them. The next day, the picture of those big boys dragging a little old lady out into the street was on every front page. And when she saw those photographers, Hazel, Mrs Viner screamed and bucked and kicked for all she was worth. I'll never forget the pictures. She made it look like the MacKenzies were killing her!'

Hazel grinned.

'Biggest mistake those boys could have made,' mused Mrs Gluck again. 'From that day forward, no one ever thought of the MacKenzie brothers in the same way. Whenever anyone mentioned them, the first thing you thought of was the picture of them manhandling a sweet old lady who could have been your own mother. Once the Centre was built, no one was prepared to move into it. No one wanted to be associated with their name. It stood empty for five long years. The MacKenzies went broke, the banks took it away from them and sold it for a fraction of its value to the Sage family. And why do you think those houses on Bentmore Square were saved? The council was so ashamed of itself that it passed a motion protecting them the very next time it met. Half the councillors had to resign as well, because of the bribes they'd taken. Mrs Viner's protest had a big effect, Hazel. Much bigger than she'd ever imagined.'

'Good!' said Hazel.

'I don't think I would have had the courage to do what she did,' said Mrs Gluck. 'I used to send her an arrangement once a month, for free, for as long as she lived, to show her how much I admired her. Just a small bouquet of freesias. That's all she ever wanted. She loved the fragrance.'

'That's a great story, Mrs Gluck. I can't believe no one's ever told me it before.'

'But don't forget, Hazel, what Mrs Viner did was illegal.'

Hazel frowned. Illegal?

'She broke the law. When she said she was prepared for the police to arrest her, she meant it. She should never have been in that attic. It *was* the MacKenzies' property. So even though people admired her for years, she was never really proud of what she did. She broke the law.'

'But she *should* have been proud!' cried Hazel. 'It wasn't fair. The MacKenzies bribed the council, you said so yourself. *They* broke the law, and so did the councillors. Why shouldn't Mrs Viner have broken it?'

'Because when someone breaks the law, you don't respond by breaking the law yourself. If someone steals something from you, you don't steal from them. You go to the police and let the law deal with it. If everyone broke the law every time someone else did, there'd be no law left at all.'

Hazel thought about that. Mrs Gluck was right. And yet so was Mrs Viner! 'So what's the answer?' she said eventually.

'There is no answer,' said Mrs Gluck. 'No easy one,

anyway. I suppose . . . well, maybe there are times when you have to go against the rules to prove your point. As long as you don't hurt anybody else, of course. But you have to be prepared to take the consequences. Mrs Viner was prepared. She was ready to go to jail, if necessary.'

'Did she?' asked Hazel.

'No. In the end, the MacKenzies didn't press charges. They already had enough bad publicity. But she *would* have gone to jail, she was ready to. And she would have thought it was right, too, because she'd broken a law, and that's what happens when you break the law.'

It still wasn't clear.

'It's complicated, isn't it?' said Mrs Gluck.

Hazel nodded.

Mrs Gluck sighed. 'I suppose what I'm trying to say, Hazel, is that if something is *so* important, and there isn't *any* other way to make your point, you might just have to do what you've been told *not* to do. But you have to be prepared to take the punishment, so it has to be something very, very important. A matter of principle. Otherwise, it's more important to do what you've been told.'

Suddenly Hazel's eyes went wide. 'Mrs Gluck! You think I should go to the party! You think I should just go without apologising!'

'Hazel, when have I ever told you what you *should* do?'

'But that's what you're saying, isn't it? That's what you're talking about.'

Mrs Gluck nodded.

'But if I want to go, I don't need to break any rules. All

I need to do is apologise to Mr Davis and say I didn't mean what I said about him.'

'And you can do that, if you want.'

'But I'd be lying,' said Hazel.

'You'd be lying,' said Mrs Gluck.

'I'd be going against my principles.'

'You would.'

'At least if I don't go to the party, I don't have to lie, Mrs Gluck.'

'But if you don't go, Hazel, everyone still *thinks* you lied. Everyone thinks you're just too proud to apologise for it.'

'So? I don't care what everyone thinks.'

'No,' said Mrs Gluck, 'you shouldn't.'

'At least I know the truth.'

'Yes, *that's* the problem. You know the truth, but no one else does. No one else knows what really happened that morning between Mr Davis and Mr Egozian. And no one else ever will. How important is that, Hazel? That's the thing we're talking about, isn't it? Is that important enough to take the risk?'

Hazel thought. She put her hands on her chin and stared at the leaves. Finally she shook her head. 'What would be the point, Mrs Gluck? I probably wouldn't even get to taste the turtle eggs before they threw me out. And then they'd be saying even worse things. They'd still say I was too proud to apologise, and now they'd say I couldn't accept my punishment either. Hazel Green is never too scared to accept her punishments, Mrs Gluck! Everyone knows that.'

Mrs Gluck shook her head. 'I don't think that's what they'll be saying, Hazel. Not if it isn't *just* you who turns up. There's someone else who's been told not to go, isn't there?'

Mrs Gluck picked up the flowers from her part-finished arrangement, and turned them this way and that, examining them.

'This isn't only about you, Hazel, is it?' she said. 'In fact, it's really about somebody else altogether. You didn't want to tell me what Mr Davis' motive was, but I think I know. I think a lot of us do. And I think we've known it for a long time. Now, I'll tell you this. Do you know why the city really got behind Mrs Viner after she showed up the MacKenzie boys? Guilt. People felt guilty about the way they'd just let the MacKenzies go ahead and destroy our history without doing anything to stop them. Finally, someone had shown the courage to stand up to them. Sometimes, when people have a lot of power, and they use it badly, that's what it takes, someone with the courage to stand up to them. That's the person who makes the difference. She's the one who shows us—'

'*Mrs Gluck! Mrs Glu*—' It was Sophie. She stopped, frowning at the strange silence in the workroom. Then she tiptoed to a shelf where there was a vase of irises, took out half a dozen yellow ones, and tiptoed out.

Hazel looked at Mrs Gluck. 'I don't know what to do.'

'You don't have to do anything, Hazel. You can just apologise, if you like.'

'I don't *want* to apologise.' Hazel shook her head in frustration. 'None of the choices are easy, Mrs Gluck.

If I apologise, I lie. If I don't apologise, I miss the party. And if I just *go* to the party, that's the worst of all! Who knows what they'll do to me then?'

The florist smiled.

'Don't laugh, Mrs Gluck. I've got to decide. And the party's only four days away. I don't know what to do. Really!'

'I know,' said Mrs Gluck. 'But you will. You'll work it out. Have courage, Hazel Green.'

21

The Yak's mother was wearing a cream-coloured gown and her fingernails were painted cream as well. Her shoes were orange. Her hair was auburn. Her spectacles had tortoiseshell frames.

She looked at Hazel. Hazel looked at the frames.

'Mrs Plonsk, if a tortoise was meant to have spectacles, it would have been given a nose,' said Hazel suddenly, at which the Yak's mother raised her eyebrows, and stared at Hazel, and was still staring when Hazel slipped past her and went to find the Yak.

'Yakov, I've made a decision,' she announced, from the doorway of the Yak's room.

The Yak was sitting over his desk, with three books open in front of him and the end of a pen in his mouth.

'Yakov, did you hear me?'

'Hello, Hazel,' muttered the Yak, without looking up from his books. 'Let me guess. You've decided you're going to start disturbing people even *more*?'

'No. That's not what I've decided.'

The Yak nodded. He was still sucking on the pen, gazing at the books. It was possible, Hazel thought after a moment, that he had already forgotten she was there.

She sat down on the bed behind him. The Yak was a strange, sensitive creature, and you had to handle him with care, just as you probably had to handle a real yak, Hazel thought. Although real yaks were used for carrying heavy loads in the mountains of Tibet, so perhaps they weren't *that* sensitive. The Yak didn't look as if he'd be much good at carrying heavy loads. Besides, even if you could get him loaded up, and even if you could get him walking, it wouldn't be long before he stopped and started thinking about some mathematical problem, even with a heavy burden weighing him down. Or he'd forget all about where he was going and get lost. Or he'd think of some formula and stop looking where he was walking, and march straight off the edge of one of those Tibetan mountains . . .

'Well?' said the Yak. He had turned around in his chair.

Hazel grinned. 'I was just thinking about you in Tibet. You wouldn't be much use, I've decided.'

The Yak narrowed his eyes. 'That's what you came to tell me? You've decided I wouldn't be much use in Tibet?'

'Don't be ridiculous, Yakov. I could tell you that any time.'

'Hazel . . .' said the Yak.

Hazel got up. She went to the Yak's violin stand and opened the music book that was resting on it. She turned the pages, glancing at each one as if she really understood all the squiggles and squaggles that were shown there.

'What does *adagio* mean?' she asked, reading one of the strange words that were written here and there amongst the squiggles.

'It means "slow". You play that section slowly.'

'Why don't they just say "slow"?'

'It's the Italian word,' said the Yak.

Yes? The Italian word? And that was supposed to be a reason?

'Can you play this?' asked Hazel, holding the book out to the Yak.

The Yak took the book. He glanced down at the page. 'Why?'

Hazel shrugged. 'Can't you play this?'

'I can play it.'

'Go on, then.'

The Yak gazed at her suspiciously for a moment. Then he got up and went to take his violin out of its case. Hazel sat down in his chair at the desk. She glanced at the three books, which were still open. The pages were covered in mathematical formulae that she couldn't even pretend to understand. She doubted she'd *ever* understand them. What she didn't know was whether that made a difference.

The Yak started to play. Hazel turned to watch him. His head was cocked, pressing the violin against his shoulder, and his eyes were closed, which was strange, thought Hazel, because he should have been looking at the music. She wondered whether the Yak was really playing the piece she had shown him, or something else altogether.

The Yak played. Eyes closed, eyebrows lowered, pointy chin pressing against the violin, arm moving the bow back and forth. Hazel wondered what was going through his mind. Perhaps nothing. Perhaps he wasn't thinking about anything. Hazel closed her eyes as well.

She tried to work out what was going through *her* mind. But it was impossible. Trying to think about what you're thinking about, she decided, is like trying to see darkness. As soon as you turn the light on to see it, it's gone.

Hazel opened her eyes. The Yak's eyes were still closed. Finally he came to the end of the piece. He opened his eyes and lowered the violin.

'Very good, Yakov,' said Hazel. 'Still, it's not really my kind of music. Too slow. Too sad.'

'But you asked for it!' said the Yak. '*Adagio*, remember?'

Hazel shrugged. 'You don't always know what you're asking for,' she said. That was one of the things her grandmother liked to say, although Hazel didn't always agree with her.

The Yak was putting his violin back in its case.

'Anyway, what I came to tell you,' said Hazel, 'is that I've decided to go to the Frengels' party.'

The Yak turned his head sharply. 'But you're not allowed to.'

'I know,' said Hazel, 'that's the whole point.'

The Yak listened to the story about Mrs Viner without interrupting. At the end of it he nodded thoughtfully.

'It's just like Konchinsky.'

'Who?'

'Konchinsky,' said the Yak. 'You must have heard of him. When Konchinsky published his paper challenging

Grueller's Hypothecated Theorem of the Prime Sequence, people said he was mad. Others said he was evil. People accused him of breaking every law. Some said he was trying to destroy mathematics entirely. And yet, Grueller's theorem *was* flawed, as we all realise now. First, it didn't fully account for the irrational prime as presented by Kugel. Second, it evaded the question of the Graussian implication. Third, it used an approximation for non-sequential factorisation.'

Hazel stared at him.

'Exactly, Hazel! Konchinsky knew it was a bombshell. Of course he knew. Why else didn't he publish for five years? He knew what the effect would be. People told him to destroy his work, to forget it. At the very least, not to publish. But he couldn't hide it forever. He knew it was right. He had to publish. Even though he knew he would suffer abuse, ridicule, hostility . . .'

Hazel was still staring.

'What?' said the Yak.

'Did this Konchinsky run the risk of going to jail like Mrs Viner?'

'Jail? What difference would jail have made?' demanded the Yak, raising a hand in the air. 'He ran the risk of being treated as a mathematical traitor. Jail's a holiday compared with that!'

Hazel sighed. 'Yes, Yakov,' she said eventually, 'Mrs Viner was just like Konchinsky.'

'*Just like* Konchinsky!' said the Yak enthusiastically.

'And now I'm going to be like Mrs Viner.'

'*Just like* Mrs Viner!'

'And you're going to help me.'

'*And I'm* going to— What did you say?'

'You're going to help me.'

The Yak shook his head. 'Hazel Green! Don't think—'

'Don't think what? You swore, Yakov Plonsk. Remember? You swore on your nose to defend the truth.'

The Yak's eyes narrowed. 'All right, I swore,' he said slowly. 'And you're going to the party . . .' he said, even more slowly. 'Where do I fit in?'

'This isn't only about me,' said Hazel. 'There are other people involved. There's no point if I go to that party by myself.'

'And you expect me to go with you? You expect to have another fight with me? In front of everyone this time? No. *No no no no no.* For your own good I'm telling you, Hazel: No! It'll just make things worse.'

'Yakov Plonsk,' said Hazel, shaking her head admonishingly. 'Always thinking of yourself. Always thinking you're going to be the star of the show.'

The Yak stared at Hazel uncomprehendingly. The star of the show? What show? He'd never been in a show in his life. It was the *last* thing he wanted.

'Who said I wanted you to come to the party?' asked Hazel. 'Did I ask you to come to the party? Did I?'

'No . . .' murmured the Yak hesitantly.

'Exactly. Next time perhaps you should wait for an invitation before you refuse it.'

'I have got an invitation. It arrived on Saturday.'

'I know. I was with Marcus Bunn when he put it through your letterbox.'

Yakov shook his head. 'Hazel,' he said after a moment, 'I have no idea what you're talking about.'

Hazel smiled. It wouldn't be a bad thing for the Yak to find out what that felt like once in a while.

'Look, you said there was no point if you went to the party by yourself.'

'True,' said Hazel.

'And you said you wanted my help.'

'True,' said Hazel.

'Then?'

Hazel shook her head. It was so disappointing. How could a boy who was supposed to be *so* mathematical, and *so* logical, jump to the wrong conclusion *so* easily? No wonder he had to keep looking things up in big thick books all the time!

'Yakov, what we have here are two . . . *premises,*' said Hazel, trying to think of words with which the Yak would be familiar. She tried to copy the tone of voice in which he usually said them. It wouldn't be a bad thing for him to see what it was like on the receiving end of that, as well. 'Do you understand so far?'

The Yak nodded uncertainly. It was just like the way she nodded when *he* was talking, thought Hazel with satisfaction.

'Now, the first premise, Yakov, is that there's someone else who needs to be at that party with me. All right?'

The Yak nodded.

'The second premise is that I need your help.'

'Exactly!' cried the Yak. 'So therefore you're asking me—'

'*Shhh!*' said Hazel, raising a finger.

'Therefore—'

'*Shhh!*' She gazed sternly at the Yak, waiting to see if he was going to be quiet. 'It does not . . . follow, that I'm asking you to go. Not necessarily. It doesn't necessarily *follow*.'

The Yak frowned. 'What else follows?'

'What else follows? This. I want somebody else to be with me at that party. That somebody isn't you.'

'Not me? You mean you'd prefer somebody else to me?'

Hazel rolled her eyes. 'Yakov, you hate parties. You never go to parties.'

'Still, it would be nice if you asked . . .' The Yak stopped. He glanced at Hazel in embarrassment.

Hazel grinned.

'Why do you need my help, then?' demanded the Yak.

'That's the first sensible thing you've said since I got here. I'll tell you why I need your help. You, Yakov, are going to convince the other person to go with me.'

22

The Yak sat against the wall of the courtyard beside Hazel. As always, it was strangely quiet here. There was hardly a sound of traffic, even though the street was only on the other side of the building. Nor was there a breath of wind.

'Are you sure he's coming?' asked the Yak for the fifth time.

'He's coming,' said Hazel. 'He always comes. Why do you think the courtyard's so clean?'

'Because no one ever comes here,' suggested the Yak.

'Just be patient,' said Hazel. 'You'll enjoy watching him when he comes out.'

'Why?'

'You'll see.'

The Yak didn't reply to that. After a moment, Hazel glanced at him. She hoped he could do the job. Hazel knew she wouldn't be able to persuade Mr Egozian to come to the party with her. From their last conversation, it was clear that the caretaker just didn't want to cause any trouble, even when he had every right to do so. But perhaps someone else, someone who had experienced the same kind of hostility that Mr Egozian had experienced, might be able to persuade him that it would be worth taking the risk. Of course, it would have been better if she could have found someone who *had* taken a risk, at least once, but the Yak would have to do. Ideally, you'd have wanted someone who fought back. The Yak only fought back in his head. But at least he did it there. At least he knew that you had to show people, even if he'd never actually had the courage to do it himself. That was what he had to tell Mr Egozian, Hazel kept saying to him as they came down to the courtyard. Mr Egozian had to show people. He had to *show* people. And what better place was there to *show* people than at the Frengels' party, when everyone would be there to see?

The Yak was looking up at the rows of windows surrounding them, climbing up towards the sky. Probably calculating how many there were, Hazel thought. No, that would be too easy for the Yak. It wouldn't take him more than a few seconds. He was probably thinking about Konchinsky. Ever since she had told him about Mrs Viner, he had been babbling on about Konchinsky. You could hardly stop him. To listen to the Yak, you would have thought Konchinsky had been as great a man as Victor Frogg, if not greater.

Hazel looked up at the windows as well. Suddenly she remembered something that had puzzled her long before. 'Yakov, you see those windows? You see how you can see through some of them, but not through others? In the others you just get reflections.'

The Yak nodded.

'Why does that happen?'

'It's got to do with the way the light hits them from the outside,' said the Yak.

'Which means?'

'Some of the light bounces off the glass when it hits

it. If enough light bounces off, that's all you see, the reflection.'

Hazel frowned. It sounded simple. Too simple.

'Is that it?'

'That's it,' said the Yak.

'Is that a rule? A Rule of Nature?'

'Yes.'

No, there must be something she didn't understand about it, thought Hazel. She just didn't know what it was yet.

A door opened. Into the courtyard came Mr Egozian, carrying his broom. He went to the corner of the courtyard, as usual, and started sweeping.

'Aren't we going to talk to him?' said the Yak.

'There's no rush. He'll get here. Just watch.'

'Why should I watch? He's just going to sweep.'

Hazel didn't reply to that. Mr Egozian *was* sweeping. Up the courtyard he went, stopped, gathered the dust up, turned around and set off again. Up and down, up and down, with his broom skimming the flagstones in a perfectly straight line. After a while Hazel glanced at the Yak. The Yak was gazing at Mr Egozian, as if hypnotised by the steady, repetitive, regular actions of the caretaker.

'Interesting, isn't it?' said Hazel.

The Yak nodded.

'You see, I told you. It's very orderly, isn't it?'

'It is,' murmured the Yak. 'It's like . . . it's like a piece of geometry. It's like a piece of geometry that's come to life . . .'

Hazel laughed to herself. The Yak kept staring at Mr Egozian.

'You remember what you have to say to him, don't you?' said Hazel. 'He has to show them.'

'He has to show them,' said the Yak.

'He has to face up to them.'

'He has to face up to them.'

'That's good.'

'Like Konchinsky.'

'No, not like Konchinsky. Concentrate, Yakov! He won't want to go. I can guarantee it. You have to convince him. You have to convince him the only way to stop Mr Davis is to face up to him, not run away. You have to tell him you experienced exactly the same thing and the only way you beat it is by showing people what it means!'

'But I never beat it,' murmured the Yak, still gazing at Mr Egozian sweeping. 'I always run away.'

'Mr Egozian doesn't know that.'

'No, Mr Egozian doesn't know that.'

'And you're not going to tell him, are you?'

'No, I'm not going to tell him,' murmured the Yak.

Hazel looked closely at the Yak. Maybe he was being hypnotised. If Mr Egozian took much longer to reach them, he was going to turn into a zombie!

'Come on. Let's go and meet him.'

Suddenly the Yak looked at Hazel. 'Now?' he said.

'Now,' said Hazel.

. . .

Mr Egozian was kneeling beside the wall, sweeping up some dust. A moment later he stood up.

'Hello, Mr Egozian,' said Hazel. 'I've brought someone to meet you. This is my friend, Yakov Plonsk. He's the mathematician I told you about, remember?'

Mr Egozian nodded. 'Hello, Yakov,' he said.

'Hello, Mr Egozian.'

'I've seen you before, haven't I?' said the caretaker. 'But you're always rushing in or out. You never stay to play with the other children.'

'Yakov doesn't play, Mr Egozian. Yakov thinks.'

'That's interesting,' said Mr Egozian. He turned and began to move across the courtyard again, pushing his broom in front of him. Hazel and the Yak walked with him. 'What do you think about?' he said to the Yak.

'Mathematics, mostly,' said the Yak.

Mr Egozian nodded. 'That's good. You must be very clever, Yakov.'

'He is, Mr Egozian. He's *very* clever. That's another reason I brought him. He wants to tell you something.'

'What's that?' said Mr Egozian.

'That you have to go to the Frengels' celebration on Saturday.'

Mr Egozian stopped. He looked at Hazel and shook his head. 'Hazel, haven't you heard? There's a new policy. I'm not invited.'

'So?'

Mr Egozian sighed. 'I've told you, all Mr Davis wants is an excuse. If I give him that, it's all over for me.'

'But the Yak's been through exactly this kind of thing, Mr Egozian.'

'Hazel . . .' said the Yak.

'He knows what it's like. That what he wants to tell you.'

'Hazel . . .' said the Yak.

'You have to face up to things, Mr Egozian. Just ask him. He'll tell you. You can't just run away. It doesn't work. You have to show people. You have to be prepared to—'

'*Hazel!*' cried the Yak. 'Do you actually want me to say anything, or should I just go?'

Hazel stopped. 'I'm sorry, Mr Egozian. I got a bit carried away.'

'That's all right, Hazel,' said the caretaker. 'I know you mean well. But there's no point. Really, Yakov, there isn't.'

Mr Egozian started sweeping again. Hazel started to follow. The Yak tugged at her sleeve

'Leave it to me, Hazel.'

Hazel started to laugh.

'Leave it to me!' said the Yak. 'Go back upstairs.'

Hazel was still laughing. But the Yak was serious. He went off to join Mr Egozian. Hazel watched in amazement.

The Yak glanced back at her. He waved her away with his hand.

Hazel went to the edge of the courtyard. She stopped to watch. Across the flagstones went the caretaker, pushing his broom, with the Yak beside him.

Suddenly she called out: 'Don't you tell him about

Konchinsky, Yakov. Mr Egozian hasn't got time for that kind of rubbish.'

'Konchinsky?' said Mr Egozian to the Yak, as he stopped beside the wall to brush up the dust.

'Yes,' said the Yak. 'He was a very brave mathematician. He's the man who challenged Grueller's Hypothecated Theorem.'

'I don't know anything about a hypothecated theorem,' said Mr Egozian.

'It doesn't matter. You know what it's like when people don't like you, don't you?'

'Yes. I know all about that,' said Mr Egozian.

'So did Konchinsky,' said the Yak.

Hazel waited in the corridor outside the Yak's apartment. 'So?' she cried when the Yak finally stepped out of the elevator.

The Yak came slowly towards her and didn't say a word until he had arrived. Hazel was almost bursting with impatience.

'He's a very nice man,' said the Yak. 'He didn't understand much of Konchinsky's mathematics, but not many people do.'

Hazel groaned.

'And he's a very orderly man. He likes order, just like me.'

'Order? Yakov, is that all you talked about, order?'

'Of course not. We talked about everything we were meant to talk about, facing up to things and showing people what they're doing. Mr Egozian thought it was very nice of you to have tried to show Mr Davis, by the way. And he thanked me for letting you shout at me. I don't think you ever thanked me, did you?'

Hazel ignored the last part. 'And?' she said eagerly, 'What's he going to do? Has he agreed to come to the party?'

The Yak shook his head.

'Yakov, you were meant to—'

'Hazel, I did everything we agreed. But Mr Egozian said Mrs Viner was lucky—'

'Mrs Viner?'

The Yak grinned sheepishly. 'We talked about her after we finished with Konchinsky.'

'Yakov, was there anyone you *didn't* talk about?'

The Yak put on a look of great concentration. 'Let me see. I don't think we talked about the Maharajah of Putt.'

'The Maharajah of—' Hazel stared. How did the Yak know about that?

'Hazel, he said he's not an old lady, like Mrs Viner. Old ladies get sympathy. No one's going to give *him* any sympathy. If he makes trouble, they'll just kick him out.'

'That's not true. Not if he makes the right kind of trouble.'

'And he said he's not young any more, either. He doesn't have the energy. If they kick him out, what will he do?'

Hazel shook her head. 'How can a person go through his whole life and never once . . . never once fight *back*?'

The Yak looked away. He didn't know who that

question was about. 'I tried, Hazel,' he muttered. 'I really did try.'

'No. You couldn't have said the right things! I should *never* have asked you, Yakov, I knew I shouldn't have. What will I do now?' Hazel demanded of herself, desperately trying to think. 'There's only two days left. I'll just have to go back to him. I'll just have to go down there and—'

'No, Hazel,' said the Yak. 'I did say the right things.'

'Be quiet, Yakov! I'm thinking. Now, where will I find him? What does he do after he sweeps the courtyard? I know! He—'

'Hazel, *you* be quiet!'

Hazel stared.

'I said the right things. He listened and he said no.' The Yak gazed at Hazel intently. 'What do you want from him, Hazel? He doesn't want you to ask him again. He told me to tell you. Don't go down now to find him. He knows you mean well, but he wants you to stop. Do you know what he said? He said: "Yakov, tell her to apologise. Tell her to go to the party and enjoy herself. I want her to do that. I'll be sad if she doesn't."' The Yak paused. 'That's exactly what he said, Hazel. The exact words.'

Hazel shook her head in disbelief. Didn't either of them understand? This wasn't about going to the party to enjoy herself! It was about something much more important.

The Yak shrugged. 'I'm sorry, Hazel. I did try, I really did. Accept it. It's over. He just won't do it. And he's not going to change his mind.'

Hazel took a deep breath. Well, that was it, then. That was it. There was nothing else she could do. But it was so *unfair*. Couldn't Mr Egozian see it? Couldn't he see that he was the only one who could help himself?

Suddenly Hazel felt as if she might start crying.

'Hazel . . .'

'I'm all right, Yakov.'

'I know you're all right,' said the Yak. 'You're always all right, aren't you, Hazel Green?'

'Yes. I am!' she said, and she turned and ran away down the corridor, before the Yak could see the tears streaming down her face.

23

The next morning, as the Moodey children walked to school, everyone was sneaking glances at Hazel Green. Only one more day! What would she do? Was she going to apologise, or was she too proud?

They glanced at her, and whispered, and glanced again.

Suddenly Robert Fischer ran in front of Hazel, jumped, spun and landed face to face with her.

'Hazel *Green*!' he demanded, putting his arm straight out and pointing his finger about a millimetre away from her nose, 'are you going to apologise or *not*?'

Hazel brushed his arm away with the back of her hand, as you'd sweep away a curtain when you want to look out a window.

'*Hazel* Green!' he cried again, and this time he jumped on the spot and landed with his feet spread apart and his two arms above his head, '*Are* you going to apologise or not?'

'Go away, Robert,' she said, and stepped around him.

But by now some of the others had stopped as well.

'Well?' said someone.

'Are you?' said another.

Hazel started to step around them as well.

'*Moodeys!*' It was the Crabstreeters, calling out from across the road. '*Moodeys!*'

'Crabstreeters all are cheaters . . .' some of the kids

began to chant, but then the taunt died away. The Crabstreeters were trying to ask something.

'Moodeys! Is she going to apologise or not?'

'What was that?' called out Hamish Rae.

'Is . . . Hazel Green . . . going to apologise . . . or not?'

Hazel rolled her eyes. The whole city seemed to know she wasn't allowed to go to the Frengels' celebration!

'Well? Moodeys! What's she going to do?'

'What *are* you going to do, Hazel?' said Mandy Furstow.

Suddenly everyone was quiet. All of the Moodey children were watching her. Across the street, every one of the Crabstreeters was watching as well.

Hazel shook her head. 'I'm not apologising. Never! It's a matter of principle. You don't apologise for telling the truth.'

'What was that? What did she say?'

'She's not apologising.'

'Never!'

'It's a matter of principle.'

The Crabstreeters were silent. They stared at Hazel. A moment later, without chanting a taunt or making faces, they began to move off.

'It's her last chance,' said Cobbler, to no one in particular. 'The party's tomorrow. Does she realise that?'

'She said "never", Cobbler,' retorted Mandy Furstow. 'Do you know what "never" means?'

Cobbler frowned, and scratched his head, wondering if *Hazel* knew what 'never' meant.

The others were still standing solemnly around her. Everyone was very quiet. For once, Leon Davis was at the back of the group. *He* hadn't had very much to say, thought Hazel. She looked at him. He was avoiding her eyes. Suddenly she had a very strange thought. She didn't know where it came from, or what made her think it. What if Leon just told the truth for once in his life? What if he just admitted to everyone what he had told her in the park, that his father really did hate Mr Egozian and all his people?

Leon looked up. Their eyes met. For an instant longer, Hazel wondered.

Then Leon glanced at Marcus Bunn. He was anxious. Suddenly Hazel understood why Leon was so quiet. He had realised that Marcus hadn't sworn to keep his secret!

Hazel glanced at Marcus as well. Marcus was watching her questioningly. Hazel knew what he was thinking. All of Leon's friends were there. Robert Fischer, Hamish Rae, all of them. Just a few words from Marcus, and . . .

Everyone knew that something was going on, but no one understood exactly, only Hazel, Marcus and Leon.

Hazel shook her head.

Still Marcus questioned her with his eyes. Hazel shook her head once more.

Leon Davis smirked.

Now he spoke. 'If Hazel's been telling the truth, why can't she prove it?' He looked around at Robert Fischer, Hamish Rae and the others. 'If she can't prove what she said, she should apologise.'

'That's right. Prove it or apologise!! Prove it or apologise!' piped up Robert Fischer.

Marcus was bursting to speak, Hazel could see it. But she bit her lip, and shook her head, and gazed at him so fiercely that he didn't dare to open his mouth.

'If she won't apologise, why *should* she be allowed to come?' demanded Leon, and he turned and walked off. Robert Fischer went with him, bouncing around at his side.

Hazel continued walking to school with the others. At first everyone was silent. But gradually, people started talking again. With only one day to go, they couldn't contain their excitement, even with Hazel right beside them. Apparently, there were going to be fried locusts. That was the latest delicacy. And this time it was Paul Boone who said it, so maybe there was a chance it was actually true.

'People eat them in Mexico,' Paul explained. 'I know because my cousin Normie went there.'

'Did he eat them when he was in Mexico?'

'I think so,' said Paul.

'I always thought Normie looked a bit like an insect,' said Alli Reddick.

'He does not!' retorted Paul, and punched her on the arm. Alli shoved him back.

'Are the Frengels bringing the locusts from Mexico?' asked Cobbler.

'Where else would they get them?'

'I don't know. There might be some people who catch them locally.'

'Cobbler!' everyone shouted. 'What difference does it make?'

Cobbler scratched his head. 'I just wanted to know, that's all.'

'I wonder how they do catch them,' said someone.

'I wonder how they cook them,' said someone else.

'I wonder what they *taste* like.'

'Crunchy, like ants.'

'So you've had ants, have you?'

Hazel smiled. It was funny when you just listened to the conversations of other people, without taking part yourself. You heard strange things. Of course, normally it was more fun to take part, but this morning she didn't feel like it.

She fell further and further behind. Soon she was by herself, and the Moodey kids were all ahead of her.

Somehow, she felt, she had ended up with the worst of all worlds. She'd told everyone she wasn't going to apologise. Even if she changed her mind, it was too late. She'd said so much about it being a matter of principle, she couldn't go back on herself now. Everyone would think she'd betrayed her principles just so she could go to a party!

Yet if she stayed away, they'd still laugh at her. They'd think she was just too proud to admit she'd accused Mr Davis wrongly. And these were the same ones who'd laugh at her for betraying her principles if she *did* apologise! Either way, she couldn't win. So why not apologise and go to the party anyway?

Because they'd be right the first time. She *would* be betraying her principles.

No, there was only one way out of it. But turning up to the party by herself was no good. That would be worse than anything. They'd laugh at her for betraying her principles, they'd laugh at her for being too proud to apologise, and *then* they'd punish her even more! If she went, it had to be with Mr Egozian. He was the only one who could show everybody how Mr Davis had treated him. Hazel couldn't do it, she'd tried that already. It *had* to be Mr Egozian.

Yet he wouldn't do it. He just wouldn't. He thought it would put his job in danger, and he wasn't prepared to do that for the sake of proving what Mr Davis had really done.

Hazel turned into the school grounds. She was late. Everyone was already inside.

It was unfair, she thought, it was so unfair. Mrs Gluck had told her to have courage, and she did. She really did. She was prepared to take the risk. It was Mr Egozian who wasn't.

But if Mrs Gluck had been with her at that moment, she might have told Hazel that taking a risk isn't the only kind of courage one can have. She might have told her that it can be as hard, and it can take as much courage, *not* to take a risk, *not* to do what you want to do, when doing it would put someone else in danger. To stick up for your principles silently, when no one knows, or cares, or even believes you, probably takes more courage than anything else.

24

As Hazel walked home from school that afternoon, Mr Frengel beckoned to her from the door of his delicatessen.

'I was wondering . . .' he said, looking around, as if he wasn't sure whether he should be seen talking to Hazel, especially if Mrs Driscoll just happened to come marching into his shop. 'Hazel, do you have a minute?'

'I've probably got more than one minute, Mr Frengel,' Hazel replied. Very few things end in just one minute, Hazel knew, especially when people say they will.

'Would you like to come inside?' Mr Frengel turned and opened the door for her.

Mrs Frengel was behind the counter, with two of her assistants. They were all serving customers. Even though it was the day before the party, the shop was crowded. On Friday afternoons, lots of people came in to get delicacies for the weekend. Mr Frengel took Hazel past the counters. As soon as she had finished with her customer, Mrs Frengel hurried to join them. Then Mr Frengel opened the door to the accounts room at the back of the shop.

They all sat down. There wasn't much space in the accounts room, and they were crowded close together.

Mr and Mrs Frengel glanced at each other for a moment.

'Would you like a fig, Hazel?' said Mr Frengel. He pushed a jar of dried figs towards her across the desk.

'Thank you,' said Hazel. She took out a fig and began to munch it. In reality, figs weren't Hazel's *favourite* kind of fruit, but it would have been impolite to refuse, and besides, you could still enjoy something that wasn't your *favourite* kind of fruit, and Hazel did.

'Have another,' said Mr Frengel.

'Thank you,' said Hazel, and she dipped into the jar once more.

Hazel ate the second fig. The Frengels were watching her. There they sat, side by side on two chairs, with their white, silky hair and their square faces and their striped aprons, like two peas that had fallen out of the same pod and landed in a delicatessen. Two quite anxious peas, to judge by the looks on their faces.

Hazel had been right at the start. This was going to take a lot longer than a minute!

She sat back and looked at them expectantly. You couldn't keep eating figs forever.

'Hazel,' said Mr Frengel at last, 'we're feeling very bad.'

'Very bad,' said Mrs Frengel, 'terrible.'

'We are. We're feeling terrible.'

'Would you like me to get the doctor?' said Hazel. 'You didn't need to give me figs, you know. I'd have gone anyway.'

Mr Frengel smiled sadly. Mrs Frengel shook her head.

'We don't mean it like that,' said Mr Frengel.

'No,' said Mrs Frengel. 'What we mean is that we're feeling terrible about you.'

Hazel folded her arms. If they didn't like her, fine. She didn't see why they needed to drag her into their shop to tell her!

'Hazel?'

'I think I should go now, Mrs Frengel.'

'Oh, no, Hazel. Please, you don't understand. We're feeling terrible that you're not allowed to come to our party.'

'Terrible. Just terrible,' repeated Mr Frengel, sighing.

Hazel nodded. *That's* what they were feeling terrible about. She almost wished she *had* gone to get a doctor. It would have been interesting to see how he could have cured that complaint!

'Hazel,' said Mrs Frengel, 'we don't know what happened between you and Mr Davis. Some people say one thing, some people say another. We say it's got nothing to do with us.'

'That's what we say,' confirmed Mr Frengel solemnly. 'Nothing to do with us. Nothing at all.'

'We've had our delicatessen here in the Moodey Building for twenty-five years. And it's been a wonderful place to have it. It's been a wonderful time. Of course, there have been ups and downs. There are people we haven't got on with so well, but what can you expect? In life, you get that. Never bear a grudge. All in all, the Moodey Building has been wonderful to us. We've been lucky. We couldn't have chosen a better place anywhere in the city, could we, Maxie?'

Max Frengel shook his head. 'We couldn't. Not even if we'd tried.'

'We just wanted to show our appreciation. We wanted to say to everyone in the Moodey Building, whether you're our best customer or you never even step inside our shop: "Thank you. Thank you to everyone. If you've got any quarrels, forget them. Come and enjoy."'

Mr Frengel nodded glumly. 'Enjoy,' he muttered.

'I'm sorry,' said Hazel quietly. 'I've spoiled it for you.'

'No, Hazel! You haven't spoiled anything. It's not your fault. Quarrels happen. Disagreements. Mrs Franchou and Mrs Gardner don't speak, ever since little Tony Franchou knocked over Mrs Gardner's dachsund with his bike. Or, as Mrs Franchou would put it, ever since Mrs Gardner's dachsund ruined little Tony's bike with its body. And how long ago was that? Twenty years. *Little* Tony Franchou is already a big grown man with three kids of his own. And still the two ladies don't talk. So? If they don't want to talk, they don't have to talk. We don't take sides. They're both invited tomorrow. They'll both come. One will sit in one corner, and the other will sit in another, and they'll be happy. That's the point. Our party was supposed to be a happy occasion. Everyone was welcome. And now, it's being used as a punishment! *We're* being used to punish you.'

'It's terrible,' muttered Mr Frengel, 'just terrible. Imagine, the Frengels' delicatessen being used to punish someone. I never thought I'd see the day.'

'The Committee tells us. The Committee *informs* us.' Mrs Frengel pulled a piece of paper out of her apron pocket and unfolded it. It was creased and smudged, as if it had been folded and unfolded many times, read and put away and read again. 'Dear Mr and Mrs Frengel. This is to inform you that Hazel Green is not allowed in the courtyard on Saturday while your celebration is in progress. She is not to be invited. If she is invited, permission to use the courtyard is withdrawn. Signed: Julius Davis, on behalf of the Committee.'

The Frengels shook their heads. Both of them, together.

'The Committee informs us.'

'What can we do?'

Hazel nodded. 'I don't blame you. I know it's not your fault.'

'If only we were holding the celebration somewhere else, they couldn't do this,' said Mrs Frengel. 'But now . . . it's too late to change it. And it's such a nice place, the courtyard. After all our years in the Moodey Building, it's the right place for our celebration. The perfect place.'

'The perfect place,' said Mr Frengel, shaking his head, as if even the perfect place had turned out to be not perfect enough.

'We're very unhappy about it, Hazel. We're very unhappy that you won't be there.'

'Mr Egozian won't be there either,' said Hazel.

'Yes, well, that's different,' said Mrs Frengel. 'Mr Egozian isn't being punished, Hazel, not like you. It's just . . . policy. He's an employee of the building. He won't be coming to the summer picnic from now on, either.'

'It's new policy, that's for sure,' muttered Hazel.

'Yes it is. It's new policy. Well . . . you shouldn't worry

about things like that, Hazel. That's why we have the Committee! They worry about policy. They know what they're doing.'

Hazel raised an eyebrow. Did they? Always?

Mrs Frengel glanced at Mr Frengel. He jumped up and left the accounts room.

Hazel gazed at the fig jar. She looked up at Mrs Frengel for a moment. Mrs Frengel glanced quickly away.

Mr Frengel came back carrying a large box. It was carefully wrapped and tied with a ribbon. He put it down on the desk.

'Here we are!' said Mrs Frengel. 'The reason we wanted to see you, Hazel, was to show we haven't forgotten about you, and to try to make it up to you, if we could. We just want you to know that if was up to us, you'd have been invited. You'd be more than welcome. We know this won't be the same as being there, but at least it's something.'

'These are some of the things we'll be having tomorrow,' explained Mr Frengel, tapping the top of the box. He smiled knowingly. 'You won't be missing a thing, Hazel. We've chosen all the special delicacies we don't normally have. Open the box tomorrow, when the party starts. That way, even if you can't come, you'll still be taking part. And I'll think of you, Hazel, and so will Mrs Frengel.'

Mrs Frengel nodded.

'Thank you,' said Hazel, 'it's very nice of you to do this for me.'

'Nonsense,' said Mrs Frengel. 'We're still hoping

you'll come, Hazel. We still hope something will happen, *something*, to end this awful quarrel in time. If it does, even at the last minute, we want you to join us.'

'I don't think that's going to happen, Mrs Frengel.'

'We're hoping, Hazel. We're still hoping.'

Hazel didn't reply to that. She looked at the Frengels. They were both watching her encouragingly, looking for a sign that their box made up for at least some of her disappointment.

And it was very nice of them. It really was. The two delicatessers knew what they were doing. If she had to miss the party, this was definitely the next best thing: a box with all the delicacies she had thought she was never going to taste!

Hazel grinned. 'Thank you,' she said again. 'This is wonderful, Mr and Mrs Frengel. It really is. Looks like I'll get to try turtle eggs after all!'

'Turtle eggs?' said Mrs Frengel.

'Of course,' said Hazel. 'Everyone's saying you're serving turtle eggs.'

'We're not serving turtle eggs, are we, Maxie?'

'No, who eats turtle eggs nowadays? There are so few turtles left, they'd die out altogether. I wonder how—' Suddenly Mr Frengel stopped. He laughed. 'It's the chocolates from Antwerp, Hilda! The ones they call turtle shells. I know what must have happened. I was telling one of the children. Now, who was it?'

'Hamish Rae?' suggested Hazel.

'That's right, Hamish Rae. He came in with his mother. That boy, he's always so impatient, I hardly had time to explain. I can't even remember what I said. Turtle shells? Turtle eggs? Who would have thought he'd take me literally? If only he'd waited to listen properly.'

Hamish Rae? Listen properly? Hazel laughed. 'Well, every Moodey kid is expecting turtle eggs tomorrow.'

'Oh, Maxie, what will we do? We can't disappoint them.'

'Of course you can,' said Hazel. 'Anyone who doesn't care if turtles die out *deserves* to be disappointed. You just have to make sure they know how the misunderstanding happened.'

'But that would be embarrassing for Hamish.'

'True,' said Hazel. 'And Leon Davis probably encouraged him to spread the rumour.'

'Do you think so?'

Hazel nodded. 'It's very likely. It's just the kind of thing Leon would do. You should make sure everyone knows that as well.' She picked up the box. It was good and heavy, and there must be lots of excellent things inside it. 'Well, I hope it's a wonderful party, Mr and Mrs Frengel, even if I'm not there. I hope it's everything you want it to be.'

'Thank you, Hazel. And we're still hoping something will happen before the party starts. We're still hoping to see you there.'

But nothing did happen before the party started, at least, not the one thing that would have made a difference.

25

By the time most people were getting up the next morning, the final preparations for the Frengels' celebration were already well under way. In various places around the Moodey Building, activity had commenced long before the sun rose. Mrs Gluck was in her workroom by four o'clock, and Mr Volio had been in the bakery all night, as usual. And the Frengels, of course, were at work in their delicatessen for most of the night, but they didn't mind, because they wouldn't have been able to sleep anyway!

Mrs Driscoll started early as well. At five minutes to eight, she appeared on the pavement outside the Moodey Building with a clipboard in her hand. Shortly afterwards a convoy of vans pulled up. As the first van turned the corner and came into view, she checked her watch and ticked off a line on her schedule. For Mrs Driscoll, the entire day would be one long series of watch-checks and schedule-ticks, and she didn't expect it to end until midnight, when she would put the last tick against the last part of the clean-up after the party was over.

The doors of the vans swung open. Men jumped out and began unloading tabletops, table bases and chairs. Soon they were marching through the lobby of the Moodey Building, into the courtyard, and out to the vans again, like a procession of crumb-carrying ants going to and from their nest. In the courtyard itself, other men were beginning to assemble the tables. They placed the large round tops on the bases and locked them in position. To Hazel, looking down from a window in her apartment on the twelfth floor, the tables looked like enormous brown mushrooms sprouting across the yard.

Later the tables were covered with tablecloths, and the mushrooms changed from brown to white.

But that was only the beginning. As the morning wore on, the courtyard got busier and busier. Long trestle tables were brought out of the vans, and were set up alongside one wall of the courtyard, to carry the food and drinks that would be brought out later. Men arrived with ladders and began fixing special rings to the walls for the bouquets that Mrs Gluck, at that moment, was making out of irises and lilies. Mrs Driscoll darted around, personally overseeing everything. As each new item arrived she ticked it off on her clipboard. Two men appeared carrying something that looked like a huge roll of red carpet. They unfurled it on the ground and Mrs Driscoll inspected it. It was a banner.

THANK YOU, MOODEY BUILDING!

The letters were so big that Hazel could read them all the way from the twelfth floor. Mrs Driscoll stood back as the men climbed a pair of ladders to fix it to the wall, and she watched them critically, calling out to them to lower or raise or straighten it a little until she was perfectly satisfied. And Mrs Driscoll, as everyone knew, wasn't satisfied easily.

Tick! Another mark on her schedule, and she turned to inspect something else that was being prepared.

There was no time for her to rest. The hours were passing, and more and more things were happening in the courtyard. People were wheeling in crates of crockery and cutlery and were beginning to lay the tables, hovering over them like bees. Men arrived with crates of drinks, and bags of ice and enormous tubs to contain them. By midday the Frengels themselves had appeared in their striped aprons, lighting up warming dishes and arranging food on the trestle tables, while all their assistants, and a few assistants' assistants, ferried more and more delicacies in from the delicatessen.

Musicians arrived and began to set up their instruments in a corner. They played a few practice tunes and the music rose all the way up the great well of the Moodey Building. Now Hazel could see a lot of other people at the windows above the courtyard, gazing down at the preparations. Mrs Gluck appeared below, with Sophie and another lady called Tilli Groner, who helped in the shop on Fridays and Saturdays. All of them were carrying armfuls of flower arrangements, the purple of irises and the yellow of tulips. Sophie and Tilli began to lay out the arrangements on the tables, while Mrs Gluck was busy with a man on a ladder, who was putting other arrangements in the rings on the walls.

And now the people really poured in! Mr Breck

arrived with a procession of waiters and waitresses. Mr Volio came in with his apprentices and trays of pastries. The Coughlins came in with their assistants and big baskets of fruit. Mrs Driscoll was literally *running* from place to place in the courtyard. The Frengels were rushing up and down behind the trestles. Everyone was hurrying and racing and last-minute-checking. And then, suddenly . . . it was finished!

The flowers were out. The tables were set. The food was ready. Mrs Gluck, Mr Volio, the Coughlins and all the assistants had left. The Frengels had gone to get changed. Only the musicians remained, sitting in their corner, and the cooks and waiters, standing in a long line in front of the trestle tables, and Mrs Driscoll, walking along the line, inspecting each one of them.

Hazel looked around at the other windows in the courtyard. Now there was hardly anyone else looking down. They were all getting ready, she thought.

Yet Hazel smiled, gazing down at the courtyard once again. She couldn't help it, even if she was forbidden to enter the scene down there. The courtyard of the Moodey Building—that old, empty courtyard where she had often gone to think in silence—had bloomed. It had blossomed. Far below, it looked like some strange, dazzling garden that glittered and glinted in the sunlight, crisp, pure and perfect, so perfect that it could last for only a few hours, and if it had bloomed that morning, by evening it must wilt.

A garden, with only Mrs Driscoll, like a hornet, buzzing around it.

The Frengels returned, wearing their best clothes. Mrs Frengel's hat was so big that, from above, it hid her completely.

Mrs Driscoll positioned the two delicatessers a short way from the entrance to the courtyard, where they would welcome everyone who came in. She said a few words to them, to encourage them and calm their nerves. And then, like a puppeteer who puts on a show but is never seen, she moved away to the edge of the courtyard, to keep watch, and direct, and make sure everything proceeded as planned.

Mrs Driscoll checked her schedule. Glancing at her watch, she raised her hand, held it there for a moment, and then let it fall. The band began to play. It was precisely two o'clock.

The Frengels' celebration had begun.

'Hazel?'

Hazel turned around.

'Are you going to apologise, Hazel? If you want to, I'll take you down to Mr Davis. It's not too late.'

Hazel shook her head.

'Are you sure?'

Hazel nodded. She was sure.

Her parents glanced at each other. Then her father turned to the mirror and began to knot his tie.

'We won't stay long,' her mother whispered.

Hazel shrugged. 'Stay as long as you like. You saw the box the Frengels gave me. I've got plenty to eat!'

'Oh, Hazel . . .'

'Come on, Miriam,' said Hazel's father. He put on his jacket. 'If she won't apologise, she'll have to learn her lesson. Now, are you sure, Hazel? We'll take you down to Mr Davis. We'll both go with you.'

Hazel shook her head. Her parents hesitated a moment longer. Then they left. Hazel turned back to the window. People were arriving. They were standing between the tables, and waiters were moving amongst them with trays. The courtyard was filling up. She saw Marcus Bunn with his sister, Susie. His parents came in just behind them. Marcus ran straight over to the tables to see the food. A lot of the other Moodey children were standing there already. Probably looking for the turtle eggs, thought Hazel, and she grinned.

She turned away. She looked at the box the Frengels had given her. She went to open it. Jars and pots were crammed inside, each with a little label. Mr Frengel had written the labels himself, with instructions on how to eat the contents. She picked one of the jars up. *Anchovies and pesto-crusted mozzarella wrapped in spinach leaves. Eat whole.* She held the container up to the light. Six little log-like things lay in the jar. Well, the party had started. Why not have a taste? Hazel opened the jar and put one of the little logs in her mouth. *Mmmm.* Interesting. Maybe a bit too salty. Maybe not. She'd have to try another one to decide! She popped a second little log in her mouth and went back to look out of the window.

Hazel tried to see if the anchovy-and-mozzarella

loglets were on the trays that the waiters were offering to the guests, but she couldn't be sure.

She sighed. She was hungry, and the saltiness of the anchovies just made her hungrier. But at the same time, as she looked down at all those people, she didn't really feel like eating. The one thing worse than being alone, Hazel thought suddenly, was being alone when you knew everyone else was together.

Suddenly Hazel smiled. There was one other person who wouldn't be down there, she was almost certain.

The Yak himself opened the door. He was holding his violin and bow in his hand.

'Hello,' said Hazel. 'I thought I'd find you here. You ought to go down to join the band if you want to play the violin.'

'I've been improvising variations on their tunes,' said the Yak.

'Really?' Hazel walked past and him and went straight into the main room, carrying the Frengels' box. 'Bring some plates,' she said.

The Yak followed her in. 'Plates?'

Hazel threw back the top of the box. 'Party time, Yakov!'

The Yak grinned.

'And you don't even have to go outside!'

'I can *see*!' said the Yak, and he grinned even more.

'Try one of these,' said Hazel, and she held out the jar

of anchovy rolls so he could eat one as he went to get the plates.

Hazel went to the window to see what was happening at the party now. The Yak's apartment was on the third floor, so she was much closer than before. She gazed around the crowd. People were starting to sit down at the tables. Suddenly Hazel grinned. There was the Yak's mother! She was wearing a shimmering purple gown, with dazzling white shoes that stood out even from this distance. Her hair was brown. She was talking to someone, and as she talked, she was waving around a pair of sunglasses with black lenses and white frames.

'Look,' said Hazel, when the Yak came back. 'There's your mother.'

'Do you know something? You were right,' said the Yak, as he looked out the window beside Hazel. 'She's started wearing spectacles. I hope they help her see better. It's funny, she never complained before.'

Hazel shook her head. The Yak! What could you do with him?

They sat down. Hazel started unpacking the jars and pots from the box. They could hear the music from outside, and there was a murmuring sound as well, like the burble of water running in a stream. People were talking, and all their voices were mixing in together.

They started to eat. The Yak, it turned out, loved salty foods, and didn't stop at anchovies. There was a jar of salted swordfish that he almost finished before Hazel even noticed. Hazel, in the meantime, was trying the cheeses, of which the Frengels had packed a large number.

'Oh, this is *good*!' said the Yak suddenly. 'What is it?' He looked at the label on the jar. '*Aubergine, chocolate and chilli paste. Spread on a cracker.* Chocolate and chilli?'

'Let me taste it,' demanded Hazel eagerly.

The Yak held out the jar. Hazel took a spoonful.

'It's good.'

'It *is* good,' said the Yak. 'It isn't logical, though, chocolate and chilli.'

'It's food, Yakov. It isn't meant to be logical!' cried Hazel, and she took another taste, savouring the strange and wonderful mix of flavours, spicy, sweet, smoky, smooth . . . She closed her eyes. Outside now, the band was still playing, and there was a tinkling of cutlery and crockery, like a second kind of music playing as well. Suddenly she thought of something. 'Do you realise, Yakov, we're the only ones here? I mean, in this whole enormous building, we're the only two people sitting inside.'

'No, we're not,' said the Yak, and he picked up the jar and took another spoonful of the strange aubergine paste for himself.

'We are,' said Hazel, opening another pot and taking a sliver of *Norse salmon stuffed with cream cheese and fennel*, according to the label. She settled back on the sofa and tasted it.

'We're not,' repeated the Yak. 'What about Mr Egozian?'

Hazel sat bolt upright. The salmon stuck in her throat. She grabbed the aubergine jar out of the Yak's hand and screwed its top back on.

'What are you doing?'

'How can you sit there? How can you just sit there like that?' demanded Hazel, throwing cheeses and jars back into the box.

'Hazel, it was *you* who came—'

'Come on, Yakov. And bring an extra plate!'

26

Amongst the children of the Moodey Building there was a legend that if you got lost in the building's basement, there were so many passages and turnings that you might never be found again. Or not until you were dead, which wasn't much better. Hazel had often heard the story when she was little, and when she was bigger she had often told it, in turn, to younger kids, which is how legends are passed on. Whether she believed it or not was another question. Right now, she wished she knew the answer!

Only one elevator went down to the basement. It was called the Goods Elevator, and it was large, chilly and plain, unlike the other elevators, which were mirrored and carpeted. The doors opened. Hazel and the Yak stepped out into a corridor, carrying the Frengels' box and three plates. There was nothing to suggest which direction they should take. The Yak looked at Hazel. She shrugged. They turned to the right. The corridor had a floor of bare concrete and walls of bare brick. The lighting was dim. There were pipes running along the ceiling and against the walls. Some of the pipes were boiling hot and others were freezing cold. Now and again there was a sound of steam hissing from somewhere. They passed big iron doors, locked with enormous padlocks. They passed staircases closed off with bolted grilles.

'His apartment must be here somewhere,' murmured Hazel.

'Logically, it must,' said the Yak.

Hazel was glad she had someone so logical with her.

'It doesn't follow, however, that we'll be able to find it.'

On the other hand, you could be *too* logical, she thought.

They kept going. Hazel didn't want to think about what would happen if they got lost. At least they had some food with them. They could probably survive on that for a day or two. If only they'd brought some drink as well. But obviously, the Frengels hadn't packed drinks, not expecting them to go exploring with their box.

There was a door! A normal door, not one of the huge iron things with padlocks. Hazel knocked. When there was no answer, she knocked again, thumping the door as hard as she could.

'Hazel?'

Hazel jumped. She looked around.

'Why are you knocking at the broom cupboard, Hazel?' said Mr Egozian, coming out of another door further down the corridor. 'Hello, Yakov,' he added.

Hazel grinned in relief. 'I've got food from the Frengels, Mr Egozian.'

'Have you, Hazel?'

Mr Egozian stood there in his doorway.

'We've come to share it with you, Mr Egozian!'

'Oh . . . Well, that's very nice of you, Hazel.'

. . .

It was stuffy inside Mr Egozian's apartment. There was a table in the main room, and a bed pushed up against one wall. On that wall, high above the bed, was a window made out of a frosted glass, and you couldn't see anything out of it. You couldn't hear any of the noise from the courtyard, either.

'You'll have to excuse me . . . this little apartment . . .' mumbled Mr Egozian. 'If I'd known you were coming . . .' He twisted his hands in embarrassment, as if he didn't know what to do next.

Hazel put the box down on the table. She began to take out the jars. 'You'll have to excuse *us*, Mr Egozian. We already started, but there's plenty left.'

Mr Egozian nodded. He stood there for a moment longer. Then he raised a finger, as if he had suddenly remembered something. 'I'll make you some tea.'

'Tea?'

'Yes. Yes, tea. You'll like it. It's sweet, with mint.' And he disappeared quickly behind a curtain that hung in front of his tiny kitchen.

Hazel glanced at the Yak. The Yak shrugged.

Hazel laid out the food, and the Yak set out his plates. Apart from the bed and the table, with its four chairs, there wasn't much furniture in the room. Hazel looked around. There weren't any pictures on the walls. There was a set of shelves but they were empty. There were a few boxes on the floor. It took a little while for Mr Egozian to come back. Hazel sneaked another piece of cheese while she was waiting.

Mr Egozian appeared with a tray and three steaming glasses of tea.

'Be careful how you hold them,' he said. 'They're hot. Hold them by the rims.' And he took the glasses off the tray one by one, holding them around the rims, to show what he meant.

Hazel waited for the tea to cool a little. When she took a sip, it was still hot. The tea was sweet, as Mr Egozian said, and it had a lovely minty aroma.

They ate. Mr Egozian didn't take much, but every time he tried something, he said how wonderful it tasted.

Hazel picked up a package that she hadn't opened yet. *'Pistachio halva. Very rich. Eat only a small slice at a time.* I wonder what that is. Pistachio halva.'

'*Chh*halva,' said Mr Egozian. 'Chhh, Hazel. You have to say Chhh.'

'Chhhhalva,' said Hazel, trying to make the sound come out of the back of her throat.

'Not bad,' said Mr Egozian.

'Chhhalva,' said the Yak.

'Good, very good.'

'Do you know what it is, Mr Egozian?'

'Do I know what it is? Chhhalva?' Mr Egozian laughed. 'Yes, I think I do. Go on, Hazel, have some. You'll like it, Hazel.'

'You have some, Mr Egozian. Show us how you eat it.'

'How you eat it? It's very simple.'

The caretaker opened the packet, which contained a block of pale material. He cut off a thin sliver from the end, and then he threw his head back and put the slice in his mouth, where he let it just melt away, with eyes closed and an expression of ecstasy on his face.

'Oh, it reminds me of my mother. The chhhalva she would make when I was a boy!'

Hazel winked at the Yak. 'Show us how you eat it again, Mr Egozian.'

The caretaker chuckled. He took another slice, a thicker one this time. Then he sliced some for Hazel and the Yak, and they ate it just as he had, letting the halva melt away in their mouth. It was sweet, and nutty, and rich, and a couple of slices would probably be more than enough.

'Do you realise, Mr Egozian,' said Hazel, 'we're the only ones inside? Just us three. The only three people in the whole of the Moodey building! Isn't that amazing?'

'I don't think so, Hazel,' said Mr Egozian. 'I heard Mrs Kaspowitz has bronchitis, and refuses to leave her bed. You know how scared she gets when she has bronchitis.'

The Yak looked sharply at Hazel. This didn't mean they had to go running upstairs to Mrs Kaspowitz' apartment, did it? It would be embarrassing—they'd eaten almost everything!

'And Mrs Lenny. She's too ill to get up. She hasn't been out of her apartment for a year. And there's Mr Kruger . . .'

'I thought they were getting a wheelchair for Mr Kruger,' said Hazel.

'They might be,' said Mr Egozian. 'They were talking about it.'

'Anyway,' said Hazel, 'even if there are five people

inside, it's still amazing, don't you think, Mr Egozian? This whole big building, where there are usually hundreds and hundreds of people, and only five inside. Think of all the empty rooms!'

Mr Egozian nodded. 'It is amazing, Hazel. It really is. Something like this doesn't happen every day.'

'No,' said Hazel. She looked at the Yak, who was staring vacantly at the empty shelves that stood against the wall. 'Look at Yakov,' she whispered to Mr Egozian. 'He's *thinking*. Sometimes he just starts *thinking* about some mathematical problem and he won't stop until you shout at him. Watch.' She grinned. '*Yakov!*'

The Yak looked up. 'I wasn't thinking,' he said. 'I was just wondering. Mr Egozian, why do you keep all your things in boxes? I was trying to work out all the possible reasons, and so far I've come up with eight.'

'Yakov,' said Hazel impatiently, 'Mr Egozian doesn't keep all his things—'

'I've been packing,' said the caretaker.

'Packing?' whispered Hazel.

'I thought so,' said the Yak. 'That was number one on my list.'

'Packing?' repeated Hazel.

Mr Egozian nodded. 'I'm getting ready to leave.'

Hazel stared at him.

'I had another . . . argument. With Mr Davis.'

'Mr Egozian, you don't have *arguments* with Mr Davis. He just shouts at you.'

'Well, this time he said he found some old newspapers under the stairs.'

'And did he?'

'Possibly. People leave them there sometimes. When I find them, I take them away. This time he found them first.'

'When?'

'Yesterday. That's the end. When the Committee meets next week, he'll make them get rid of me. I can't stop him. It's true, the newspapers were there and I should have removed them.'

'But you can't check under the stairs every five minutes!'

'Of course not. He knows that.'

'Tell them! Tell the Committee.'

'They know already. Mr Davis wants to get rid of me and he won't stop until he's done it. If it isn't this, it will be something else. Every day I have to worry about what he'll find next. I'm sick of it. Who can live like this? I don't have the strength. I'm tired. He's won, Hazel. He's won.'

'But you said you weren't going to give up! You said you wouldn't open the door for him.'

Mr Egozian shrugged helplessly. 'I'm tired.'

'Where will you go?' said Yakov.

'What? Oh, I'll go to live with my daughter. She's always telling me I should come to live with her. I've always thought that's what an old man would do, and I'm not an old man. I didn't think I was, anyway. But maybe I am.'

The Yak shook his head.

Mr Egozian smiled sadly. 'At the moment I feel old, very old. Maybe it's hard for you to understand.'

Hazel wasn't sure if it was hard to understand, because she wasn't even thinking about it. As Mr Egozian had been talking, she had begun to think about something else. And it was much more interesting! Suddenly she grinned.

'You think it's funny?' said Mr Egozian.

'No, Mr Egozian. Now *you* don't understand.'

'What?'

Hazel jumped up. She could barely contain her excitement. 'Mr Egozian, if you're leaving, you've got nothing to lose.'

'So?'

'So? You've got *nothing to lose*.' Hazel glanced meaningfully at the ceiling. The courtyard, where the Frengels' celebration was taking place at that very moment, was probably directly above their heads.

Now Mr Egozian did understand. 'No, Hazel. No. I'm not . . . I'm not a troublemaker. I've never been a troublemaker.'

'Neither am I!' she cried. 'But sometimes—'

Hazel stopped. The Yak was laughing. Even Mr Egozian was grinning.

'What? What is it?'

'Oh, nothing,' said the caretaker,

Hazel glanced severely at the Yak, who tried to put on a serious face.

She turned back to the caretaker. 'Sometimes you've just got to make trouble, Mr Egozian. Sometimes, if something's important enough, it's the only way.'

Mr Egozian shook his head. 'It's just not me. It's not the way I am.'

'Mr Egozian, you *have* to do it. This is your chance.'

'To do what, Hazel? To do what? To get my job back? I don't want it.'

Hazel shook her head. 'This isn't about your job, Mr Egozian.'

'Then what is it about?'

'Truth,' said Hazel. 'And fairness. This is your chance, Mr Egozian. To fight back, to show them. *This* is your chance.'

The caretaker gazed at the girl in front of him. She was on her feet. Her eyes were ablaze. Her fists were clenched in anticipation.

He sighed. 'Truth? Fairness? I'm sixty-eight years old. I stopped hoping for that a long time ago.'

'No!' exclaimed the Yak. He jumped up as well, breathing heavily, trembling with passion. 'You must never stop hoping for truth, Mr Egozian. Never!' he cried. 'Remember Konchinsky!'

'That's right! Remember Konchinsky!' cried Hazel.

The caretaker shook his head in disbelief. Now they were both on their feet, both of these children. What did they want from him? He felt too old, too tired for this.

'Mr Egozian, I'm not allowed up there either,' said Hazel. 'But you already know that I'll go, if you will.'

'And I will too, Mr Egozian,' said the Yak, his voice shaking, barely rising above a whisper. 'I'll be with you every step of the way.'

27

In the courtyard, the waiters were clearing plates away from the tables. Mrs Driscoll watched them with an expert eye. They weren't the fastest waiters she had ever seen, but they weren't the slowest, either. As they finished, Mrs Driscoll glanced towards the band leader. He was waiting for her signal. She nodded. The band leader turned to his drummer, and the drummer commenced a drumroll.

The people at the tables stopped talking. There were a few last voices, and then there was silence.

Mr Frengel looked towards Mrs Driscoll. She nodded at him. Mr Frengel stood up. He looked pale and nervous. Everyone was watching him. He walked towards the microphone that was set up in front of the band. When he got to the microphone, he stopped, coughed a couple of times, and then hesitantly began his speech.

Mrs Driscoll was still standing at the edge of the courtyard, where she had spent most of the past two hours, directing proceedings with nods and gestures and waves of the arm. She hadn't tasted a single one of the delicacies that everyone else had been enjoying. She wasn't there to enjoy herself. She was there to organise! Besides, for Mrs Driscoll, organising *was* the most enjoyable thing in the world.

She listened to Mr Frengel. He was saying how much he appreciated all the kindness people had shown him in his years at the Moodey Building. The usual thing, thought Mrs Driscoll, who must have listened to ten thousand speeches in her career as an organiser.

Mrs Driscoll glanced at her watch. On the whole, she was quite satisfied. They were only four minutes behind schedule, and she always built in at least ten extra minutes for delays. After the speeches Mr Volio's pastries and all the sweet delicacies were going to be served, and after that there was going to be dancing to the music of the band as evening fell. As Mrs Driscoll knew, no one wants to sit around listening to speeches when they're having a good time, especially when there's dessert and dancing to look forward to. But you simply have to have them. It's an impossible balancing act that every organiser faces! All you can do is keep the speeches short and get the dessert quickly onto the tables, and as an experienced organiser, that was exactly what Mrs Driscoll had planned.

The Frengels had each been allocated five minutes to speak. After that Mr Davis was going to reply as head of the Residents' Committee. He had been told to stick to five minutes as well, but Mrs Driscoll privately had allocated ten minutes to him in her schedule. And whether he would limit himself even to this was the thing that concerned her. Inevitably, Mr Davis would speak for exactly as long as Mr Davis wanted, as he always did, which was usually a lot longer than anyone else would have recommended.

In fact, this was the only thing worrying Mrs Driscoll. Everything else had gone so smoothly, people had been talking and laughing during the meal, the food was excellent, the music charming, the atmosphere warm. There was no reason to suppose that the dessert and dancing wouldn't live up to the same standards. The Frengels' party, Mrs Driscoll could see, was well on the way to being remembered as one of the most wonderful days in recent Moodey history, for which she would be modestly prepared to take the credit. Barring something totally unexpected, like two guests getting into a fight and smashing the band's guitars over each other's heads—an 'episode', as an organiser would say, which is every organiser's greatest dread—a long, boring speech from Mr Davis was about the only thing that could spoil it.

Mrs Driscoll looked at the microphone again. Mr Frengel had already finished. She checked her watch. Three minutes. Mrs Frengel was making her way up, dwarfed under her enormous hat, looking even more nervous than Mr Frengel. Mrs Driscoll smiled encouragingly. Mrs Frengel coughed and stuttered as she began. She had a little card in her hand and she kept glancing at it. She said how much she appreciated being part of the Moodey family, how much she appreciated getting to know all the people who lived in the building, how much she appreciated . . . More appreciation, thought Mrs Driscoll, just like the first speech. Mrs Driscoll smiled to herself. They really were humble people, the Frengels, and they spoke simply. Yet was there really anything more to say? Anything important? Often those were the most touching speeches, the simple ones, which people remembered. And at least there wasn't time to get bored! Mrs Frengel's speech was over in three minutes as well.

And now it was time for Mr Davis . . .

Mr Davis marched towards the microphone. When he reached it he stopped and carefully adjusted it to his height. *He* had made a few speeches in his time, you could see, just from the way he arranged the microphone. He cleared his throat. Mrs Driscoll looked apprehensively around the crowd. People were already fidgeting. A few people rolled their eyes. Others looked at their watches, to see whether Mr Davis would beat the thirty-eight-minute record he set when he got up to say 'a few words' at last summer's picnic.

He did beat a record. But it wasn't the record for his longest speech, it was the record for his shortest.

'Ladies and gentlemen, boys and girls . . .' he began, pausing almost at once to gaze meaningfully around the Moodey population that was seated before him, 'as the Chairman of the Residents' Committee, the Residents' Committee of the Moodey Building, the building in which Victor Frogg was born, Victor Frogg, ladies and gentlemen, the Father of Our Nation . . .' he paused, gazing meaningfully again, 'as Chairman, I repeat, of the Moodey Residents' Committee, it gives me great pleasure to stand before you today and to have the opp—'

He stopped.

Mrs Driscoll frowned. Mr Davis was known for his dramatic turns of phrase and eloquent delivery, but it was an unusual delivery that required him to stop in the middle of a word. And to stop for so long . . .

People were glancing questioningly at each other. To what? To have what opportunity?

But apparently Mr Davis didn't want to tell them. Instead, he was just staring, straight ahead, at the entrance to the courtyard.

Slowly, people began to realise that they were witnessing something unprecedented. For the first time that anyone could remember, Julius Davis had stopped in the middle of a speech!

Heads began to turn to see what had caused this. Soon everyone was looking at the entrance.

Three people stood there. Around the courtyard, there were gasps of surprise. Seeing the strange boy who lived on the third floor, and who never came out except to go to school, was an event in itself. And most of the people knew that the caretaker hadn't been invited. But *everyone* knew that Hazel Green had been banned!

Mrs Driscoll looked at the newcomers, then at Mr Davis, then at her clipboard. She ran her eye frantically over the carefully arranged schedule, although Hazel Green's appearance wasn't listed on it, nor was there anything about what should be done if it happened . . . and Mrs Driscoll knew it already, since she had written the schedule herself!

Now people were looking at Mr Davis again. Still he hadn't said anything. They looked back at the three arrivals. They hadn't said anything either. They didn't even seem to know what they were meant to be doing.

And they didn't. Hazel had no idea. Her mind had been so occupied with the idea of *going* to the party, she hadn't actually thought about what to do once she got there.

But they couldn't just keep standing. Hazel took a step forward, and nudged Mr Egozian to go forward as well.

When Hazel thought about it later, she couldn't remember a single face, a single sound from those moments when she walked towards Mr Davis at the microphone. Yet people were watching her, they must have been. And somewhere in that crowd were her parents, and Mr Volio, and the Yak's mother, and Mrs Gluck, and everyone else she knew from the Moodey Building. And maybe she did look around, and maybe she did see some of them, only she couldn't remember it later. Later, those few awful moments of silence, as she walked forward between the tables, would seem as if disconnected from everything else in the world, as if she didn't even breathe once, as if she were advancing along a tunnel in which time stood still, where there was nothing around her, not even the surface of the ground beneath her feet, only the image of Mr Davis, his face going red with anger, waiting for her at the end.

Suddenly she heard the sound of heels clattering across the flagstones. Out of the corner of her eyes she saw Mrs Driscoll coming towards them, clutching her clipboard under her arm. But then a thundering, booming voice stopped Mrs Driscoll in her tracks.

'No, Mrs Driscoll. *I'll* handle this.'

Mr Davis had forgotten that he had the microphone in front of him.

'That's far enough!'

His voice was so loud, amplified so strongly by the microphone, that it came out as a roar. People frowned, shocked. The smaller children covered their ears.

'That's far enough, I said!'

Hazel had stopped. Mr Egozian was beside her. And on the other side of Mr Egozian was the Yak. He had promised the caretaker he would go with him to fight for truth, and he was keeping the promise, although his heart was beating so quickly it felt as if it were about to take off and flutter right out of his chest.

Mr Davis' voice exploded out of the microphone again.

'Hazel Green. Leave the courtyard. You had your chance to apologise.'

'I didn't come to apologise.'

People strained to hear. After Mr Davis' booming voice, they could barely make out Hazel's words.

Mrs Driscoll was frozen in horror. The girl was starting an 'episode'! She was starting an 'episode' right in the middle of Mrs Driscoll's event.

Mr Davis' face was going redder.

'Leave! You're spoiling this day for the Frengels and everyone else.'

That was a bit of an exaggeration, thought Hazel. If Mr Davis had gone on with his speech, no one would even have noticed they'd arrived. But what was she going to do now? Maybe she should lie down right there, on the flagstones, and make Mr Davis come and drag her away. If only she'd remembered to phone the newspapers first!

'And what about me, Mr Davis? Should I leave also?'

Oh no, thought Mrs Driscoll, the caretaker's getting involved in the 'episode' as well!

Mr Davis stared haughtily at Mr Egozian, as if an *employee* of the building didn't even have the right to ask him a question.

And what would have happened next, Hazel didn't know. It couldn't have gone on like this forever, with Mr Davis booming at them from the microphone. Yet any number of things could have happened, and the 'episode' could have ended in any number of ways. The thing that *did* happen, seemed to happen only because, just at that moment, Mr Egozian did something.

It was only a gesture. But gestures can be interpreted in different ways, and a gesture that means one thing to one person may remind another person of something else entirely.

Mr Egozian held out his hands, palm upwards, beseechingly, towards Mr Davis.

Mr Davis stared. Suddenly his eyes blazed—not as before, but differently, with anguish, with terrible rage. Anyone looking at him could see that something had happened. That gesture had triggered something in his mind.

He roared, utterly forgetting the microphone in front of him.

'You!'

At the tables, people stared at him in shock. Adults were covering their ears as well now.

'I know what that means! You! Is that what you want? More money? Is that what will make you go at last? But it's never enough! You never have enough, do you? Like all your kind. It's still not enough! Now what, Tudarian? My shoes? My shoes? Is that what will satisfy you? All right, my shoes, then. *Take them!*'

And Mr Davis swept aside the microphone, which fell with an ear-splitting shriek, and ran towards the caretaker.

'Oh my!' squeaked Mrs Driscoll, and fainted.

Mr Davis had stopped and was working feverishly at his shoelaces, hopping first on one leg and then on another, despite his great height and bulk, like the boy of eight he had once been. Still he couldn't get his shoes off fast enough, and he almost toppled over in the attempt. Yet now they were off and he ran the final few steps towards Mr Egozian in his socks and then he stopped and hurled the shoes at the caretaker, one after the other. And one after the other, the shoes hit Mr Egozian in the chest and fell at his feet.

'There,' cried Mr Davis. 'Now, go! Go!' His voice cracked, and then his shoulders slumped, and then he looked around, as if noticing for the very first time that four hundred people were watching him, and he buried his face in his hands, like a boy of eight, standing in his socks on the flagstones of the courtyard that the caretaker had swept so often.

And Mr Egozian, who hadn't flinched and hadn't moved even an inch to protect himself from the shoes, gazed at him for a moment, and then he turned and walked away. And Hazel turned and went with him, and the Yak went with him as well. And Hazel would never forget the dignity of the man in front of her, the simple caretaker who lived in the tiny basement apartment, the straightness of his back and the measured pace of his steps, as he walked between the tables, past the silent, staring people, away from the sound of Mr Davis sobbing behind him.

———

28

'He left yesterday, Mrs Gluck,' said Hazel, sitting in the florist's workroom with Marcus Bunn a few days later. 'He said he just didn't have the heart for the job any more.'

Mrs Gluck nodded. She examined a group of yellow carnations lying on the table, looking for the ones that had just the shape and colour she wanted.

'He could have stayed. The Committee all came down and said they wanted him to stay. They brought Mr Davis with them and he apologised. He apologised to me as well, Mrs Gluck. He came upstairs and said sorry!'

'Did he?' whispered Marcus Bunn, his eyes wide with amazement.

'Of course he did!' said Hazel. 'What do you think?'

'*You* wouldn't apologise,' said Marcus.

'I had nothing to apologise for,' retorted Hazel, and she shook her head, and gave Marcus the kind of glance you give someone who ought to understand certain things by now, and if he doesn't, he ought to find someone else to explain them.

'But you *never* apologise,' muttered Marcus. 'About *anything*.'

'I'm sorry, Marcus, but I do,' said Hazel, and she turned back to Mrs Gluck. 'He said that after everything that had happened, Mrs Gluck, he just didn't want to stay. The thing is, it wasn't Mr Davis. It was everybody else.'

'Yes,' said Mrs Gluck. She selected three of the yellow carnations and then picked up a pair of bright orange gerberas.

'When people found out he wasn't invited to the party, no one seemed to be bothered. A few people came up to him and said they were sorry, apparently, but most people didn't even do that. Even the ones who were sorry said they couldn't do anything about it. According to them, it wasn't anyone's fault. It was policy.'

'What *is* policy?' demanded Marcus. 'No one will tell me!'

'Policy, Marcus, is something that lets you be horrible to someone else and pretend there's nothing you can do about it,' said Hazel with an air of authority.

Mrs Gluck smiled.

'That's when he realised that people didn't care, Mrs Gluck. They just didn't care about him. He'd been here all these years, but as far as they were concerned, he was just a stick of furniture. All these years he'd lived and worked here, and in the end that's what he was, a stick of furniture. So he said it was time to go to his own family, who really do care about him. He's going to live with his daughter and his grandchildren.'

Mrs Gluck nodded. She added a fourth carnation to the arrangement she was making, and then twisted twine around the stems to bind it together.

'I don't understand why no one cared, Mrs Gluck. I just don't understand.'

Mrs Gluck got up to put the arrangement in a vase. Then she turned around and looked at Hazel.

'People cared, Hazel,' she said quietly. 'I told you before. I think a lot of us suspected what was going on.'

'Then why didn't anyone do anything? Why didn't anyone at least say something!'

'Hazel Green, not everyone's like you.'

Hazel laughed. She knew that! Personally, she didn't think it would be such a great thing if everyone were. It would be a pretty chaotic world, that's for sure! The Yak wouldn't be happy.

Mrs Gluck sat down. 'What I mean, Hazel, is that most people aren't very brave. Not everyone's a Mrs Viner. We might think something's wrong, really think it's wrong, yet we don't say anything about it.'

Hazel stared at Mrs Gluck. 'But I *always* say what—' She stopped. She glanced at Marcus. Marcus flushed red as soon as he saw her looking at him.

'Hazel Green,' said Mrs Gluck, 'sometimes I think you're the most thoughtful girl I've ever met . . . and sometimes you don't seem to understand the one thing that's as obvious as the nose on your face.'

Hazel frowned. Suddenly her nose felt itchy, and she scratched.

'It needed someone with courage,' said Mrs Gluck.

'It wasn't just me, Mrs Gluck. The Yak came as well.'

'Yes. He was brave, wasn't he?'

'No, he *wasn't*!' muttered Marcus Bunn. 'He just walked behind you. He didn't even say anything. And he was invited, anyway. He was *supposed* to be there.'

'I don't think Mr Egozian would have agreed to come with me if the Yak hadn't been there,' said Hazel, ignoring Marcus, who was still muttering about *anyone* being able to do what the Yak had done.

Mrs Gluck nodded. She was silent for a moment, consulting her order book. Then she looked up at Hazel and Marcus again. 'I had a customer once who was a famous mountain climber,' she said. 'Have I ever told you about him? Earnest Collins, his name was. He was probably the bravest man I ever knew. Nothing could scare Earnest Collins. The stories he used to tell! Anyway, one year, while he was waiting to go on an expedition, he started to get bored. So he decided he'd climb the Moreton Tower just for a stunt. You know how tall the Moreton Tower is. Anyway, up he went, with half the city watching and cheering from below. There was only one thing everyone forgot. At the top of the Moreton Tower, at that time, was the antenna that broadcast radio for the whole city. It was attached to a special mast that went even higher in the air. And when he got to the top of the tower, instead of stopping, Earnest Collins went up that mast as well, using his hooks and his ropes. Everyone cheered like mad. You should have seen it, the mast swayed like a reed. It was frightening just watching it, really. Earnest Collins managed to climb it, of course, but he also managed to put one of his hooks straight through the antenna wires. Every radio in the city went dead. Like *that*!' Mrs Gluck snapped her fingers. 'It took two days to fix it, and another week before everything was back to normal.'

Hazel and Marcus gazed at the florist.

'The point is,' said Mrs Gluck, 'it's not enough just to be brave. You've got to know what to do with your courage, when to use it. You've got to know when something is really worth striving for. Otherwise, you'll just end up putting your hook through an antenna, and no one will thank you.'

'Mrs Gluck,' said Marcus, 'is that really true?'

'Why shouldn't it be true?' said the florist. 'Earnest Collins!' Mrs Gluck shook her head, chuckling. 'When he wasn't on an expedition, he used to come in once a week to buy flowers for his mother. Chrysanthemums, he liked to buy her, although she really liked lilies. I could never convince him to change. Once, when he didn't have time to visit her himself, he asked me to send the flowers, and I sent lilies instead. Oh, I felt very naughty. Next week he came in and said his mother hadn't stopped thanking him for the flowers he'd sent and could he have the same ones again please. That put me in a spot!'

'What did you do?' said Marcus.

'I told him the truth. At first he wasn't very happy. He looked at me with a grim expression. I'll never forget it. It took a long time for him to accept that he'd been wrong to keep buying chrysanthemums. That can be one of the problems with brave people. A lot of them have a habit of thinking they're always right.'

Mrs Gluck and Marcus both looked at Hazel.

'Well, at least I don't have that problem!' said Hazel.

'Of course not,' said Mrs Gluck.

'*Nooo*,' said Marcus, shaking his head solemnly.

'That's Mr Davis. Mr Davis has that problem,' said Hazel.

'*Had*,' said Mrs Gluck. 'I think he's learned a lesson.' Mrs Gluck got up and went to collect flowers for her next arrangement.

'Why do you think he just went mad like that?' asked Hazel. 'What happened?'

Mrs Gluck shrugged. 'Who knows? Who knows what goes through someone's mind? There was hatred and resentment there that had built up since he was a boy. It just burst out. It's not so easy to lay blame, Hazel. There's always a reason.'

Marcus frowned.

'Well, I messed up the Frengels' party, that's for sure,' said Hazel. 'It was meant to be their big day, and it turned out to be a disaster.'

'No, people enjoyed themselves,' said Mrs Gluck.

'Before I turned up, they did. No one looked too happy afterwards.'

'That's true,' said Mrs Gluck. 'No one felt like dancing after you left. I was looking forward to having a waltz with Mr Lamberto.' And she winked at Marcus, who flushed red all over again.

'You see! I *did* ruin everything!'

'You didn't,' said Mrs Gluck firmly. 'You didn't ruin anything, Hazel.'

'But it was meant to be perfect. The Frengels planned it for weeks.'

'Mrs *Driscoll* planned it for weeks,' muttered Marcus.

Mrs Gluck chuckled. She picked up a large apricot-coloured tulip. 'Do you know what this one's called, Marcus?'

Marcus shook his head.

'Song of Eden,' said Mrs Gluck.

'*Song* of Eden? But it's not a song, it's a flower.'

'Exactly,' said Mrs Gluck. She looked at Hazel, who was staring at the leaves on the worktable. 'You shouldn't worry, Hazel. You really shouldn't. The Frengels wouldn't want you to, and neither would anyone else. I'm proud of you. There are people who'll never say it to you, but they're glad you did what you did.'

Hazel glanced at Marcus. Marcus nodded.

Hazel shook her head. 'But it was the Frengels' twenty-fifth anniversary. It was meant to be a day people would remember forever!'

'People *will* remember it,' said Mrs Gluck. 'Think of it like this, Hazel. It might have been just another party, but you've given us something else to remember.'

ODO HIRSCH

grew up in Melbourne, Australia. After living in London for many years, he returned to Australia, where he continues to write full-time. In addition to the Hazel Green books, he is also the author of a series about an intrepid explorer named Bartlett. The three Bartlett adventures have all been chosen as Junior Library Guild selections.